COWBOYS OF THE BOX R

A Clay Jared Western

R. Annan

Cowboys of the Box R
Copyright 2015 by R. Annan
Edition 1.1
WGA Reg. #: R31601 (9/29/15)

Photography © L. Annan

One Vision Publishing
ISBN: 978-1-942338-39-0 (eBook)
ISBN: 978-1-942338-38-3 (Print)

Other Western books by R. Annan:
Fight for the Lazy M
The Gunfighter in Winter
Long Ride to Hell's Kitchen
Owl Hawks
Gunfight at Barfield Springs
Shootout at Sanctuary City
Last Days of a Gunfighter
Red Bandana
Copperhead Moon

To Laura

1.

Haverston Junction was a small cattle town thirty miles south of Wichita, Kansas. On Friday nights the ranchers came in to relax, have a few drinks, play cards and shoot the bull at the Haverston Junction Gentlemen's Club.

On winter nights it was a good place to be when the cold January wind blew blankets of snow down Haverston's main street. Stray dogs and cats slinked about in the alleyways looking for a warm place to curl up, but there wasn't much to find as the alleys were where the coldest winds blew.

Inside the Gentlemen's Club things were far from cold, as at a certain table a heated discussion between four ranchers was in full swing. It concerned an upcoming bare-knuckle match between Sammy Dalton and George Barry in Kansas City.

"No, no," rancher James Restin said. His English accent seemed out of place in this small western town. "Barry will take Dalton in ten."

"What, rounds?" asked Lazy S rancher Bill Slocum.

"No, minutes, Bill!" Restin insisted. "Minutes!" His voice was heavy with whiskey.

"What's so special about Barry, Jim?" Running B rancher Ed Bell asked.

"Yeah, Restin, what's so special about Barry?" Len Farrow of the Circle F wanted to know. He was just as intoxicated as the Englishman.

"Because he's English and Dalton is, is, well, he's not!" Restin said haltingly, slurring his words.

"Irish," Farrow insisted. "Barry is Irish."

"All one and the same, Lenny, old chap," Restin insisted. "All one and the same." Restin belched. "Pardon me."

Restin was known as a nice fellow who had a good bit of money but knew nothing about cattle ranching. He and his sister had come into the area from London. They'd bought a small ranch, put their brand on it and left the running of it to their ramrod, Stoker McGraw, and his cowboys.

"You wouldn't like ta put some money on Barry, would you, Restin?" Ed Bell asked.

"Sure, Ed," Restin replied all too quickly. "If you want to lose your money, sure." He chuckled.

"How about we say five double eagles," Bell said. "I don't want ta go too hard on ya, Jim."

"Don't worry, Ed," Reston replied. "You won't win. Why, my man, Punch Elliot, could take Sammy Dalton in one round!"

No one noticed a tall man with cotton-colored hair who was sitting alone at the next table listening. He got up, came over to their table and stood smiling down at them.

"Colonel Denvers," Bill Slocum said. "How do you do, sir?"

"Gentlemen!" Denvers replied. "I've been listening with interest to your conversation. Especially to Mr. Restin's remark about his man, Punch Elliot. And I was thinking perhaps we could do a little gentlemanly wagering in that area."

Restin had only met Colonel Denvers a few times and had rarely spoken to him. Once the Colonel asked him if he'd had enough of cattle ranching and was interested in selling the Box R. Restin had said no.

"I'm not sure I know what you mean, Colonel," Restin said.

"You were saying that your cowboy Punch Elliot was a tough one, were you not, Restin?"

"Punch Elliot? Yes. He was once a bare-knuckle boxer," Restin said with pride. "At least that is what I've heard. And by the looks of his face I believe it to be true." Restin chuckled. "It's pretty well smashed in."

"Then he must be as tough as you say."

"I'm confident he is, Colonel."

"What if we got up a little bout between your fellow and one of mine?"

Restin replied, "Sure, why not? It might prove interesting and good sport to boot."

"How confident are you in your man's ability as a boxer, Mr. Restin?" the Colonel asked.

"Considerably confident, sir."

"I see," Denvers said. He took a cigar out of his coat and lit it. The man had a cold, humorless way about him. "Considerable enough to put some money on him?"

For a moment the Englishman was taken aback. He suddenly felt as if the Colonel was leading him down a path he didn't want to go down. He had bragged about how good Punch Elliot was and now he was stuck with it.

"Of course," Restin heard himself saying with bravado. "As much as you'd like, Colonel."

"As much as I like?" the Colonel asked, as if pleasantly surprised, as if these weren't the exact words he was hoping to hear.

"Yes. As much as you like, sir," Restin repeated.

The Colonel looked at the others to make sure they were listening and following the conversation. He took a draw on his cigar and blew out a billow of smoke. When he had everyone's attention, he spoke.

"Ten thousand, Mr. Restin?" It was more of a challenge than a question.

A heavy quietness fell over the group. The Colonel stared off across the room as if bored, waiting for Restin to make a decision. The Englishman was silent, at a loss for words.

"That's what I thought," Denvers chuckled sarcastically. "All bark and no bite." He started to walk away.

"Alright," Restin blurted out.

Denvers stopped and turned back. "Are you sure, Restin?"

The Englishman nodded. "Yes. I'm sure."

"We could make it five, if ten is too high."

"No, no, ten is fine."

"Will you shake on it, Restin?"

Without getting out of his chair, Restin reached up and shook hands with Denvers. That sealed the bet. A handshake was as binding as a contract and the Englishman was well aware of that. There were three witnesses at the table who had watched it all happen.

"When do you want to do this?" Restin asked.

"Well, I'm a bit busy right now," Denvers said. "Why don't we leave the details to our ramrods? Let them figure out when and where. We don't even have to be there. They'll tell us who won. There's no rush, is there?"

"No, of course not," Restin said. He felt relieved. It sounded like the Colonel wasn't taking this too seriously. In fact, he had been rather casual about setting up the fight. Maybe he'd forget all about it in time.

Later, as he rode back to the Box R, James Restin had worrisome thoughts. If he lost the bet, how could he pay up? He couldn't ask his father back in London. His father had pleaded with Restin not to abandon his job at the family's law firm and rush off to the wild, savage West to buy a ranch. The old gentleman was even further crushed when Restin convinced his sister Erica to go with him.

As he rode into the yard, Restin glanced down at the Box R bunkhouse. It was still lit up, although most of the cowboys were in town this Friday night. He wondered if he shouldn't go talk to his ramrod, Stoker McGraw, and tell him about the bet.

The thing was he seldom found reason to talk to McGraw except on paydays. Very few words passed between them. The cowboys were, for the most part, an uneducated lot of rough-and-tumble fellows who fought, swore and drank that horrible whiskey they called rotgut. They carried guns and sometimes shot each other over the slightest insult.

7

They thought more of their horses than they did of themselves. And worst of all, they hated to take a bath.

As for Erica, she was fascinated with them and even invited them in to her small library and talked about books.

Restin walked his horse down to the barn, unsaddled, fed and watered him, then put him in the corral. As he walked back to the ranch house he saw a light on in Erica's library. She liked to read in the evenings.

A cold wind followed him up the porch and into the house.

"Is that you, James?"

"Yes, Sis."

"Finished for the night, are you?"

"Yes. I'm rather tired, dear. I'm turning in now."

"Nighty-night, James. Sleep well."

Restin sighed and walked up the stairs to the bedroom. He knew he wouldn't sleep much that night.

2.

Colonel Frank Denvers had fought for the Union in the Civil War. He served under the command of Brigadier General George D. Wagner. At the Battle of Nashville, Wagner's Division was in front of Army Commander Major John M. Schofield's Army of Ohio. In that position Wagner's forces took the brunt of attacks by General John B. Hood's Confederate Army of Tennessee.

On November 24th, Wagner's forces were well forward of the lines but were forced to pull back and hold between Spring Hill and Columbia. It was during this withdrawal that Colonel Denvers and his men were cut off. In a short, savage battle they were captured by a select group of English volunteers who had joined General Lee's Army.

It was later said that at least ten thousand Englishmen had come across the ocean to support and fight for the Confederacy for various reasons. Colonel Denvers would come to hate them all as a group.

Colonel Denvers, Lieutenant Merkle and First Sergeant Malone were sent to Blackshear Prison, Georgia, with other Union prisoners.

As the inflow of captured Union soldiers grew by the thousands, Blackshear soon became over-crowded, and Denvers, Merkle and Malone were transferred to a place called Andersonville, also in Georgia.

Originally opened in February of 1864, Andersonville was meant to accommodate about ten thousand Union prisoners. It quickly became overwhelmed as over four hundred Union prisoners a day were squeezed in. By the end of June, it had 26,000 prisoners. Two months later it had 33,000 prisoners.

The camp deteriorated quickly and became full of filth. Men wore rags and food was scarce. Ultimately, 45,000 Union soldiers were stuffed into an area meant for 10,000 men. By the time the war ended, 13,000 had died of disease, poor sanitation, malnutrition, overcrowding and exposure to the harsh elements.

When they closed Andersonville in April of 1865, Denvers, Merkle and Malone were among the survivors. They hardly resembled human beings, but they walked out with their heads held high and a bias against the British who had captured them.

The Colonel and his two trusted followers went north for a while only to find it had changed too much for their tastes. The woman that the Colonel was engaged to had gone off with another man, leaving him very bitter. After a year he decided to go west.

Denvers had a fair amount of money and figured he would buy a ranch and make a living raising and selling cattle, which was popular at that time. Merkle and Malone went with him.

No man would ever have two more loyal followers than Merkle and Malone. Denvers made Merkle ramrod of the Triangle D and Malone his second in command. The two ran the ranch with an iron fist. Over a period of time they became to be known as Dutch Merkle and Mongoose Malone, so called by the cowboys who had the habit of giving every cowboy they met a nickname that fitted him.

Merkle was seen as stingier than a Dutchman, although some said he was tighter than a crab's ass. Malone was seen to be faster than a mongoose, quick-tempered, and having a face only a mother could love. The Colonel came in for some scrutiny, too. He was seen as rigid and humorless and had a back stiffer than a washerwoman's ironing board.

So said the cowboys of the Triangle D.

3.

It was a cold, stiff November afternoon when the new man rode through the front gate into the yard of the Box R Ranch. The first thing that struck him was how normal things were. Dogs, chickens and cats were wandering around just like on every other ranch he worked for. It was comforting. The place had a feeling of hominess.

As he stopped to pull his hat lower and the collar of his coat higher against the bite of the wind, he glanced over at the white, two-story clapboard house. For a moment he thought he saw a curtain move. Someone was watching him.

He sized the place up quickly. There was the usual barn behind the house, a corral with horses attached to it and a windmill with a trough a few feet away. A cistern pump was near the back porch of the house.

The smell of stew drifted up from the bunkhouse. The stranger saw an ancient cast iron stove under a canvas tarp next to it. An old cowboy limped about tossing vegetables into a large pot atop the stove. A fire blazed inside the stove's firebox. He glanced up at the intruder, nodded and then kept working.

More food lay on a small table near the stove, and there were three long tables with benches next to it for outside eating under a large lean-to.

The new man tied his horse and went into the bunkhouse. It had cots for fifteen hands. There was a door to the ramrod's room in the far wall. One of the two cowboys lying around noticed the stranger and got up from his bunk.

"What kin we do fer ya, friend?"

"He's a lookin' fer Stoker," the other cowboy said.

The stranger nodded. "Is the boss in?"

"In there," the first cowboy said then shouted. "Hey Stoker! We got a new one fer Punch!"

For some reason they both laughed as if they had just heard a joke. The door to the ramrod's room opened and two men came out.

The first man was a towering giant with broad shoulders and coal-black hair. His face was weather-worn to a rough, grainy, leathery texture. Two blazing, dark eyes stared out beneath a heavy forehead. The nose was bulbous above a wide, grinning mouth. He swaggered when he walked and smiled with confidence. He came straight at the new man as if to run him down, but stopped short of it.

The other man was much shorter but stockier and more muscular. His brown hair was thin except for shaggy tufts on the sides of his bullet-shaped head. His ears had that cauliflower malformation of a boxer. Old scars dotted the landscape of his beaten face, mostly around the eyes, cheeks and chin. Even his lips were scarred from old wounds.

"I'm Stoker McGraw," the tall one said. "This is Punch Elliot, my second. What kin we do fer ya, stranger?"

"The man at the Cattlemen's Association said to give you this," the newcomer said.

He dug a chip out of his pocket and gave it to McGraw. It was a pasteboard the size of a double eagle and it had a Box R brand on it. The big ramrod took the chip.

"What's yer name?"

"Jared. Clay Jared."

"Where'd ya work last?" the big man asked as he walked a circle around Jared.

"Paxton's Circle P. Down in Winfield County."

"Why'd ya leave?"

"He had to cut back. Sent three of us packing."

"Too bad," McGraw said. He gave Jared the once-over again then nodded. "Twenty a month is what we pay."

"Sure," Jared said. He knew what was coming next.

"We got three line camps, west, north, an' east," McGraw began. "I rotate the men out there every two weeks, so you'll git ta do thet a few times a year. You okay with thet?"

Jared nodded.

"I keep some men right here ta help the cook an' do some carpenter work an' odd jobs, too. Kin ya swing a hammer an' hit a nail?"

"Tolerable," Jared said. "Though I've been known to bust a thumb now and then."

That remark seemed to break the ice and they all laughed.

"Yeah, me too," one of the cowboys said. Punch Elliot didn't seem to know what they were laughing about.

"Oh," McGraw said. "I don't know ifn they told ya, but this is the Restin's spread. They're from over there. A place called Englin."

Jared nodded.

"They sorta keep ta themselves. Hell, you might never even see them unless ya hitch up the buckboard fer 'em. But they're damn fine people," the ramrod said. Jared said nothing in response to that. "So, go ahead and stow yer gear. It's getting' near ta suppertime. We'll talk more later."

Just as they were about to walk away, Punch Elliot put a hand on McGraw's arm.

"Ya didn't tell him about tha line dance, Stoke!"

McGraw smiled at Jared.

"Oh, yeah," the big man said with a grin. "I forgot about thet. We have this little thing fer new fellahs. It's sorta what they call an initiation thing. Sort of a welcome ceremony. I'm sure yer gonna git a big kick outta it, Jared."

McGraw and Elliot turned and walked away laughing. The two cowboys went back to their bunks with big smiles on their faces.

Jared wondered why.

4.

Clay Jared went outside, got his saddle and gear, brought it into the bunkhouse and dropped it on an empty cot. He then walked his horse down to the barn, talking softly to it. He fed and watered it and gave it a good brushing down. Finally, he put it in the corral.

"See ya later, pal," the cowboy said, rubbing the horse's neck and ears. It nudged him against the corral fence. Clay chuckled. "Be good. Don't cause no trouble."

Just as Jared was returning to the bunkhouse, eight cowboys came pounding in, hollering and hooting after a hard day's work. They were covered with range dust and looked tired. He followed them into the bunkhouse. They shook hands with Jared, shooting their names at him so fast he couldn't remember them all.

The odd, out-of-the-ordinary ones were easier. Pages Henry, Charcoal Bradley and Tonsils O'Toole stuck in his mind and stayed there. Not so much Tug Grimes, Red McBride or Cory Ogden.

They ate supper at the tables out under the open shed next to the kitchen alongside the bunkhouse. It was the basic son of a gun stew with sourdough biscuits followed by an apple raisin tart and coffee. The hot food soon cooled in the cold January air. It had to be eaten quickly.

McGraw told Jared that Restin's sister actually did all the cooking and cleaning in the big house. Their taste in food was different than the cowboys and they ate at different hours, too.

"Most times ya kin smell her cookin' in the evenin'," McGraw chuckled. "It sure makes yer mouth water."

Later, after Jared had stowed his gear under his cot and was lying down, McGraw and Punch Elliot came out of the back room and stood in the center of the bunkhouse.

"Gather 'round, fellahs," the ramrod said with a smile.

Everyone got up and stood facing McGraw.

"Taday, as ya all know, we got us a new cowpoke by the fancy name a Clay Jared," McGraw said. "An', as we always do, we put new fellahs through the line dance. Ain't thet right, boys?"

"We sure do, Tug," someone yelled. That was followed by a chorus of "We sure do!"

"So give us some room here, men, and we'll git this little dance a started."

Everyone backed off a few feet from Punch Elliot who stood with his hands on his hips smiling like a bear that had just eaten a bucket of honey.

"Now, Jared," McGraw said, "take yer shooter off. You won't be a needin' it fer this little number."

Everyone laughed. Jared shrugged, unbuckled his gun belt and tossed it on his bunk.

He came back to McGraw who pointed down at a line cut into the planks of the bunkhouse floor. Punch Elliot was facing the line, about a foot back from it. He had a joyous look on his face, like a child about to receive a toy.

"Now," McGraw explained, "the real name of this here game is called 'Blow the Man Down.' It's a little game we use ta play while I was a stoker on a paddleboat on the Mississippi River, in me younger days. I taught it ta Punch here after we met, an' we've made a pretty penny from it ever since, right, Punch?"

Punch Elliot nodded and chuckled. "We sure did, Boss." He looked around nodding with pride.

"But them days is behind us an' now here we are havin' a little fun playing 'Blow the man Down,'" McGraw said. He smiled at Jared. "Alright now, here's how ya play the game, Jared. You hit Punch right in the kisser as hard as ya kin, see? If Punch's knees even so much as buckle, you win the game."

"Ah, win what?" Jared asked. Everyone laughed.

"Ya win not getting' hit by Punch, an' thet's the end of it."

"What if his knees don't buckle?"

"Wal, then he gits a crack at yer pretty kisser, my friend."

"What if I'm not inclined to play?" Jared asked.

There was a deep, almost embarrassing silence. Everyone waited for the ramrod's answer.

"Wal, it don't go like thet, ya see," McGraw said flatly with a half-smile. "Ifn ya wants ta ride wif the Box R brand ya gotta be a Box R cowpoke. An' the only way yer gonna be one is to dance the line, Jared. So what's it gonna be? In or out?"

"I see," Jared said.

The cowboy stared at the massive hands at the end of Punch Elliot's arms. Elliot was smiling at him as if to say, "Aw, come on. Hit me!"

Jared shrugged and said, "I'm in, Boss."

Cheers went up from the crowd. Punch Elliot reached out to shake Jared's hand. The new man felt the tremendous strength in Elliot's huge paw.

"Okay, now," McGraw continued. "You ready, Jared?" Jared nodded. "Then let it rip."

Elliot stood smiling as he faced Jared, his arms at his side, waiting anxiously. The cowboy selected a point on the man's jaw, inhaled, and swung a roundhouse right with all the force he could muster. It connected solidly with a loud crack at the base of Elliot's jaw. Elliot's head twisted sideways on its thick neck, paused for a moment, then slowly turned back into place.

He was still smiling and his knees never even twitched.

Jared never saw the return blow coming. There was a blur of movement, a jolting crack and everything went white then black. The next thing he knew he was sitting on the floor seeing double and wondering where he was.

Pages Henry and Charcoal Bradley lifted him up on his feet. The others patted him on the back.

Punch Elliot came over and shook his hand. "Yer a good sport, Jared. A damn good sport. An' ya got a good punch, too."

Tonsils O'Toole handed him a bottle. "Have a drink, Jared."

Jared grabbed the bottle and took a long pull of rotgut. It burned like fire all the way down.

Stoker McGraw stepped in. "Jared, you did well. You took a good punch. Yer a Box R man now." He shook Jared's hand. "Put 'im ta bed, boys."

Pages Henry and Charcoal Bradly helped Jared over to his bunk. O'Toole came with the bottle and they all had a few more pulls together, emptying it.

Finally, Jared lay back and fell asleep.

5.

Two days after the line dance, Stoker McGraw sent Pages Henry, Charcoal Bradley, Tonsils O'Toole and Jared up to the north line shack as part of a swing drive.

It was a two days ride through pine trees, aspen and birch, with a lot of open switch grass in between. On the first day they passed the branding site and then the herd being moved in for marking. The further north they went the fewer cattle they spotted. Finally, they saw only scattered groups. That was where the north line shack was.

They unloaded the packhorse and hobbled their mounts in a small area by a stream that had winter grass.

"We'll take her easy for a day then go look for outliers," O'Toole said.

The shack had a simple hearth with a grate for cooking. Henry went out and came back an hour later with a wild turkey. Jared helped pluck it and Henry kept the downy feathers for a pillow. They had a can of beans, hardtack and coffee with it. For dessert they opened a can of peaches.

The next day they went to work. Henry rode east, Bradley rode west, and O'Toole and Jared went north. The plan was to sweep all the strays into the center and take them ten miles south to a pick-up point where Tug Grimes, Red McBride and Cory Ogden would consolidate them and move them down to the branding site.

They spent twelve hours a day in the saddle out in the cold, sometimes sleeping in the saddle instead of on the hard ground, or not sleeping at all. It was then that Jared learned why the cowboys called O'Toole Tonsils O'Toole. He sang in a beautiful Irish falsetto that seemed to soothe the cows. They were especially attentive when the cowboy sang "The Wind That Shakes the Barley" and "Down by the Glenside."

Whenever they had idle time, which wasn't often, Pages Henry would take out a book he had in his saddlebag and read while Charcoal Bradley drew pictures in a sketching book he kept handy. Sometimes they played cards or checkers.

It got colder each day and harder to find strays. The snow was gathering in the higher hills and sometimes sheets of it blew down to them. At night the wind hit the line shack.

One day Jared and O'Toole followed a set of tracks in the snow and came upon a mother and her calf near a dead briar patch by some big rocks. The calf had gotten into the patch and couldn't get out. Its mother was standing by, calling to it.

"I'll get the little bugger," O'Toole said and dismounted. He had on his heavy chaps so he wasn't worried about the needles.

Just as he got near the calf, Jared heard a fierce growl. A mountain cat made a leap and came sailing from a high rock. It was almost atop O'Toole when Jared fanned off three quick shots, hitting it in the air. It was dead by the time it knocked O'Toole flat on the ground into the briars.

The shots scared the mother cow and she ran off a few yards but stopped to look back at her baby. Jared dismounted and helped O'Toole up.

"Damn," O'Toole said. "That was some shootin', pard."

"Come on, I'll help you with the calf," Jared said, reloading his Colt.

Between the two of them they freed the calf. It ran bawling to its mother and they both went off.

"You want the skin?" O'Toole pointed at the cat.

"No, it's yours if you want it," Jared said.

"I'll take it, then," O'Toole said. "The meat's too tough to eat. I'll leave it for the coyotes."

"Yeah. They'll be fighting over it before the night falls. By morning it'll be gone," Jared said. O'Toole nodded.

They laid the cat out on the frozen ground and went to work skinning it. It was almost dark by the time they got back to the line shack.

One day Jared asked Pages Henry what book he was reading.

"It's called '*Moby Dick*.'" Jared laughed at the title.

"What's it about?"

"This fellah has a go-around with a white fish big as a barn. He's tryin' ta corral this bugger 'cause it bit his leg off at the stump."

"You're kidding me, right?" Jared laughed.

"Nope! Here look!"

Pages Henry showed Jared several pictures.

Jared nodded. "Let me know how it turns out."

"I sure will, pard." Pages Henry said.

One day Jared caught Charcoal Bradley drawing his picture in his sketch book. Later he got a chance to look through it and saw Bradley had also drawn all of the Box R cowboys. It seemed his forte was doing portraits, and they were some of the best Jared had ever seen.

They kept bringing the strays down to the pickup point. Finally, there was nothing to do but go south to the branding site and help out. They spent another week there. The herd was left to scatter out again until the spring roundup, and the cowboys headed home after over a month of range work.

Most of them had a fully grown beard and needed a bath and a good time in town, which Tug McGraw made sure they all got.

"Boys, it sure looks like this spring we're gonna have the biggest herd yet fer the drive ta Ellsworth. An' they'll be a bonus in it fer everyone."

Suddenly all the hard work seemed worth it.

6.

A day after the range work was over, Stoker McGraw called Clay Jared into his room. Punch Elliot, Tug Grimes, Red McBride and Cory Ogden were at the table drinking and smoking. They greeted him with a smile and a handshake.

"You wanted to see me, Boss?"

"Yeah, Jared. Sit down. Have a snort."

Jared sat down next to Ogden and took a short pull on the bottle just to be sociable.

"What's up?" Jared asked.

"You been pullin' yer weight pretty good around here, Jared, and me an' the boys appreciate it. An' pottin' thet mountain cat up thar was pretty neat. I like thet."

"Thanks."

"But the reason I called you in is because a deal is comin' up concernin' the Box R, an' it smells mighty fishy."

"What sort of a deal, Boss?" Jared asked.

"I jest got a message from Dutch Merkle, the ramrod of the Triangle D sayin' thet Denvers and Restin have a bet on."

"What kinda bet?"

"Thet his man can beat the tar outta Punch."

Jared nodded. "How much is the bet for?"

"The pot is fer ten thousand dollars."

Jared whistled and pushed the brim of his hat back.

"Wow! That's pretty steep."

"It sure is, an' I think the Colonel has an ace up his sleeve."

"So you don't trust him?"

"Not him nor Dutch or Mongoose Malone, fer thet matter," McGraw said.

"He wants ta do the fight tonight at the Black Latigo Saloon."

"Where's the Black Latigo?"

"About five miles out from here on the old Caldwell ta Ellsworth coach trail," the ramrod said. He stopped, rolled a cigarette, watching Jared's eyes as he did so. "I'd like ta have you go along jest in case it turns ugly, if ya git my drift."

"Why me, Boss?"

"O'Toole says yer faster than greased lightning."

Jared chuckled. "I ain't that fast, but I can hold my own."

"I ain't askin' ya ta start nothin'. I jest want ya ta be there in case Merkle decides ta pull a fast one." McGraw lit the cigarette. "But it's up ta you, ifn you'd rather not."

"No, no, Boss," Jared said quickly. "Count me in."

The big ramrod broke out into a wide, happy grin. They all patted Jared on the back.

"No more drinkin', boys," McGraw said. "We gotta be sharp fer ta-night." He put the cork back in the bottle. "Be ready ta ride in two hours."

Grimes, McBride and Ogden left but the ramrod held Jared back. He noticed that Punch Elliot seemed to be looking off in the distance with a sweet, fixed smile on his scarred lips.

"Listen, Jared," McGraw said in a low, confidential tone. "I want ya ta keep an eye on Dutch Merkle. Thet bastard is up ta somethin' here. You can bet with ten thousand dollars on the line the Colonel has a surprise up his ass."

"Alright," Jared said.

Jared went back to his bunk and lay down. It was Friday night and most of the Box R cowboys were in town except for him, Grimes, Mc Bride and Ogden. He was asleep when McGraw and Elliot came out to get him.

"Let's ride," the big ramrod growled. He was anxious to get it over.

In an hour they came up on a rise and stopped to look down at the Black Latigo a half mile away. It was an old stage stop that had been converted into a saloon.

"Ah, jest so ya know, Jared, as a rule we don't go there.

"Why not, Boss?"

"It's mostly Triangle D territory."

"I see. That's good to know."

They rode down, dismounted and tied their mounts to the hitching post rail next to a dozen Triangle D horses. McGraw waited a moment and walked up the steps onto the porch with the others following. He glanced over at Jared to see where he was, nodded and walked through the batwing doors.

It took a while for Jared's eyes to adjust to the flickering light of the oil lamps that hung from the rafters. He noticed the bar to his right where several Triangle D men stood drinking. At the tables were more. There were also some women in the mix. An off-key piano tinkled in the back by the rear door. The place smelled of stale tobacco juice, rotgut whiskey and sweat.

Dutch Merkle came out of the shadows, a girl hanging on his arm. He pushed her away and handed her a double eagle. She pouted and left. He chuckled and adjusted his gun belt.

"Hi, Dutch," McGraw said.

"Hi, Stoke," Merkle said. "I see ya got my message."

McGraw nodded. "That's why we're here, Dutch. Ta settle it fair an' square."

Merkle smiled and nodded. "Yep. Fair an' square, Stoke." He glanced over at Punch Elliot and laughed.

"What's so funny, Dutch?" McGraw asked.

"You'll see real soon, Stoke," Merkle chuckled.

"What the hell are ya pullin', Merkle?" McGraw growled.

Without answering, Dutch Merkle snapped the fingers of his left hand and a thin little man came out of the shadows. He was pale and long black hair hung over his shoulders. His face was very feminine and he was dressed in the tights of a ballet dancer and a white silk shirt with frills. On his feet were black shoes with metal heels and pointed metal toes.

The man was a French foot boxer, one of the deadliest sports in the world.

"Meet Frenchy La Quah from Baton Rouge," Merkle chuckled.

McGraw had no idea what a French foot boxer was and never noticed the footwear. He burst out laughing.

"Frenchy La who?"

"La Quah," Merkle repeated.

"What's the joke, Merkle?"

"No joke, McGraw," Merkle said. "In fact, I'd like to make it interesting with a little side bet."

"Oh, ya would, huh?"

"Yes, How about five double eagles?"

"Hell, yes! Make it ten, ifn ya wants ta!"

"Alright," Merkle said. "Ten it is. Shake on it?"

"Sure."

McGraw reached for Merkle's hand and they shook.

"Give them some room, men!" Merkle shouted. He waited a moment. "Okay, that's good." He turned and smiled at Frenchy La Quah. "He's all yours, Mr. La Quah."

Merkle laughed hard as he backed away to give the boxers more room.

The Frenchman smiled at Punch Elliot and motioned for him to come on. The big man quickly closed the gap between the two and threw a swift right uppercut at La Quah only to hit air. The little man's body seemed to be made of rubber as he nimbly dodged like a cat to avoid the blow.

"Voilà, mon ami!"

Elliot lurched forward and tried to nail the Frenchman with a flurry of left and right jabs, but each time he missed as he swerved and twisted out of reach, laughing and taunting Elliot in his own language. They went around in circles with the Frenchman backpedaling as if on wheels. His footwork was mesmerizing.

The big man finally ran out of steam and stood panting in place.

"Come here, ya little son of a bitch!" Punch Elliot gasped, sucking in air.

Frenchy La Quah walked up to Punch Elliot, spun like a top on one foot for a few seconds, then kicked him square in the groin. The big man grabbed himself and sank to his knees groaning in pain.

The Frenchman spun around for a second time and delivered another blow to Elliot's chest with the heel of his right shoe. This shot took the wind out of Punch Elliot's lungs, causing him to gasp like a fish out of water. A third blow followed, this time to the side of Elliot's chin. It struck with such force it snapped his head back with a cracking sound.

Punch Elliot let out a big sigh and fell forward, hitting his face on the plank floor. He lay there groaning in pain as the Frenchman smiled and stepped back to admire his work.

"Sweet Jesus!" Stoker McGraw muttered, staring down at his friend.

Dutch Merkle sneered. "Finish him off, La Quah!"

The Frenchman walked slowly up to where Punch Elliot lay twisting and turning, trying to get up. Elliot looked up, chuckled, then spit a mouthful of blood at La Quah, splattering his pretty white shirt.

"Kill the bastard!" Dutch Merkle screamed.

With a sneer on his face, the Frenchman pulled his right leg back. Just as his foot flew forward Elliot came alive. He caught La Quah's shoe in his enormous left fist and held it fast as he got to his feet.

The crowd roared as Punch Elliot raised his left arm and held the Frenchman flopping about like a hooked fish. Then he did a little round dance himself and swung La Quah crashing into the bar. There was a sickening sound as the Frenchman's head smacked against solid wood and he fell limp on the floor with one hand in a spittoon.

"You son of a bitch!" Dutch Merkle bellowed like a wounded whale. He drew his gun and shot Punch Elliot, hitting him in the shoulder. He took aim again for a second shot.

"Hey, asshole!" Jared shouted as he jumped to cover Elliot who was down on the floor holding his arm.

"Who the hell are you?" Merkle growled.

"I ride for the Box R, and I'm calling you a no good Yankee son of a bitch!"

Jared drew from a crouch just as Merkle fired. The Triangle D man's bullet took a chunk out of Jared's coat collar. The Box R man fanned off three rapid shots into Merkle's body. He jerked three times, spun sideways and dropped like a cut-down tree.

That started the dance.

Grimes, McBride, Ogden and McGraw all drew their guns and lined up near Jared. The bartender pulled out a double-barreled scattergun and fired a blast into the wall facing the bar.

"I got one more ifn anybody wants it!" He shouted. "Now take yer scurvy asses outta my saloon. Right now!"

Everyone put their guns away. Grimes and Ogden grabbed Punch Elliot and helped him up and out to his horse.

"When the Colonel learns of this, the shit is gonna hit the wind," Grimes said.

"Ta hell with thet bastard," Ogden said. "Thet was a dirty trick he tried ta pull back there."

"Yeah, it weren't right," McBride said.

"You alright, Punch?" McGraw asked.

The big man was holding his arm. Jared got alongside him on the right and McGraw got on his left.

They rode slowly back to the Box R.

7.

There were reasons why Colonel Frank Denvers wanted to get hold of the Box R Ranch but foremost was his dislike for James Restin and his sister. They were English and Denvers hated the English. Because of them he had been captured in the Civil War and sent to Andersonville Prison and almost died. In his mind, the Restins were still the enemy.

After the incident at the Black Latigo Saloon and the killing of Dutch Merkle by Restin's men, Denvers was more bitter than ever. He promised himself he would destroy James Restin financially or physically, preferably physically.

After considering several options, he decided on a simple and legal way to accomplish his goal.

He sent word to Restin, on the pretense of paying him the ten thousand dollars they had bet, to meet him at the Gentlemen's Club in Haverston Junction. When James Restin arrived the Colonel was already at the bar drinking. It was a Saturday and the club served early.

"Hello, Colonel," Restin said. "You wanted to see me?"

Restin was in a good mood because he was expecting to leave with a ten thousand dollar bank note in his pocket.

"Hello, Restin," the Colonel said dryly.

"Well, it looks like I was right. My man did win, didn't he?"

"Ah, actually no, he didn't," Denvers said.

"What do you mean he didn't?" Restin was astounded.

"Well, as I heard it, the Frenchman knocked Elliot down and out."

"Down, yes, but not out. Elliot got back up quickly and finished the fight. My men saw it happen, old chap."

"Well, they lied to you, Restin," Denvers insisted.

Restin stared at Denvers for a moment not believing what was happening.

"Are you saying you're not paying up, Denvers?"

"No. Your man lost, therefore you owe me."

"I protest, sir!" the Englishman said. "You're reneging on your bet! That's dishonorable and I won't stand for it, Denvers!"

The Colonel stood towering over the smaller man. "Is that a threat, Restin?"

Restin was too upset to answer. He sputtered, searching for the right reply but found none.

"How's that pretty sister of yours, Restin?" the Colonel suddenly asked.

"What?"

"I said, how is that pretty little sister of yours?"

"My sister?" Restin was stunned. "What does she have to do with anything?"

"I hear she's popular with the Box R cowboys."

The Englishman couldn't believe what he was hearing.

"Leave my sister out of this, sir!"

"I hear she's pretty intimate with some of the men," the Colonel snickered.

"You go too far, sir!"

"I also hear that she is partial to saddle bums, as well."

"How dare you, sir!" Restin yelled. The room suddenly went silent. "Take that back, Denvers!"

Denvers smiled maliciously and said, "I don't care to, Restin." He held his hand over his mouth and pretended to yawn as if he was bored.

"Then I shall have satisfaction, sir!"

Restin removed one of his leather gloves and slapped Denvers across the face with it. It wasn't a very hard slap and Denvers chuckled.

Rancher Bill Slocum came over to join them.

"What's going on, Restin?" Slocum asked.

"Colonel Denvers has insulted my sister. I demand he retract it and apologize."

"Go to hell, you English bastard," Denvers said sharply. "And take that bitch sister with you."

"You will answer for that remark, sir!" Restin was seething with anger.

Several other ranchers saw what was up and gathered around.

"Any time and any place, Restin," the Colonel said coldly.

"Right here and now, sir!"

"Fine," Denvers said. "Here and now suits me just fine."

"Very good," Restin heard himself saying in an angry voice he didn't recognize as his own. Inwardly he was very frightened.

"I'll be your second, Jim," Bill Slocum said.

"Thank you, Bill," Restin replied looking around as if lost.

From that moment on things seemed strange to the Englishman. He moved as if in a stupefied daze. One moment he was standing at the bar in the Gentlemen's Club and the next minute he was out in the dueling field behind it, where matters of honor were settled by club rules. He was holding a dueling pistol that seemed to be much too heavy and he was sweating in the cold January air, even though he had taken off his coat and hat.

Someone was explaining the rules to him and the next thing he knew he was counting off fifteen paces to the east as Denvers counted fifteen paces to the west. It seemed like the last step came too quickly. He turned and wiped his eyes with his free hand, trying to locate Denvers. His knees were shaking badly. Finally, he saw Denvers. The Colonel was a tiny figure miles away, it seemed.

Suddenly something slammed into the Englishman's chest. It was followed by the sound of thunder and a very white light.

Marshal Tolliver was notified. The lawman and his deputy hitched up the buckboard. They got the body of James Restin and took it out to the Box R Ranch.

8.

The next day Erica Restin had the Box R cowboys assist her in the burial of her brother, James Restin.

While several of the men chipped away at the frozen ground in a field behind the ranch house, the cook and Jared made a fine cedar box. They wrapped the Englishman's body in a wool blanket, placed it in and nailed the top shut.

When word came that the hole was finished, they carried the casket out of the house and carefully lowered it into the hole. Erica read from the Psalms as the cowboys took a handful of dirt and dropped it into the hole. When it was filled she read James Restin's favorite psalm from the Bible.

When she was finished she announced that Tonsils O'Toole would sing James Restin's favorite song:

> *"Alas, my love, ye do me wrong,*
> *To cast me off so discourteously.*
> *And I have loved ye so very long,*
> *Delighting in your company.*
> *Green sleeves was all my joy,*

Green sleeves was my delight.
Green sleeves was my heart and soul,
Who but she tonight..."

It started to snow. Crows watched from the birches at the edge of the field, cocking their heads to one side, as if listening to the pure, golden tones of O'Toole's voice. A wind caught the branches and shook the crows took off in a rush of wings. They circled once and came to rest again.

The Box R boys spent the rest of the morning placing a short white picket fence around the site, leaving room for one or two more. After that they ate apple and raisin tarts and drank coffee in the kitchen with Erica. She complimented Tonsils O'Toole on his fine voice.

All the cowboys were very polite and did not drop any swear words.

A day later Erica Restin went into her brother's den, sat at his desk and went through all its contents. James had handled all the accounts, including the cattle books, ranch inventory book and other accounts. She found everything in order until she came to the credit and debit ledger.

It was there she discovered the Box R Ranch was on the brink of being insolvent. It was running a deficit mainly caused by her brother's withdrawals from the savings account. There were no clues as to where the money went but Erica assumed it had gone to pay gambling debts at the Gentlemen's Club and other pleasures at the Half Moon Saloon and the Haverston Junction Hotel.

Erica sat at her brother's desk in shock. She was now sole owner of a ranch in Kansas that was dead broke. It had no operating funds and the cowboys were expecting to get paid in a week. She felt like crying but burst out laughing instead.

There was nothing else to do except tell the cowboys how things were. Most likely they would walk off, and she wouldn't blame them. Poor James. What a stink he had left her in.

Finally, she got her shawl, walked outside on the porch, stared down at the bunkhouse and waited. A cowboy soon saw her and ran in. A moment later Stoker McGraw came out to her.

"Ma'am? Yer gonna ketch yer death a cold out here, standin' around like thet."

Erica walked down into the yard to face him.

"Mr. McGraw," she said, "I'd like to talk to the men."

"In the bunkhouse, ma'am?"

"If I may."

"Give me a second ta git 'em all in proper form, ma'am."

The ramrod hurried into the bunkhouse. Erica could hear him yelling orders about getting their clothes on and putting out their cigarettes and making up their bunks. In five minutes he escorted her in. They were sitting at attention on their bunks, waiting for her. She stood a few feet inside the door and smiled.

"Men," she began, "first of all I want to thank you all again for the lovely burial you gave James."

They all said, "My pleasure, ma'am."

"But what I want to tell you is that it appears the Box R is almost out of operating funds. I don't have enough money to pay any of you this month and probably won't until after the drive to Ellsworth this summer."

Tonsils O'Toole said, "Ma'am, did you know thet Colonel Denvers owed yer brother ten thousand dollars?"

"No, I didn't, Mr. O'Toole. Where did you hear that, if I may ask?"

Stoker McGraw stepped in. "Ah, it's a bit complicated, ma'am. But it's true. There was some bettin' goin' on between the Colonel an' yer brother. Yer brother won flat out."

"Did that concern the shooting at the Black Latigo with Mr. Elliot getting shot and Mr. Merkle killed?"

"It did, ma'am."

"I see." Erica heard about the fight from James, but not about the wager. Knowing this now, she figured he had kept it a secret, probably intending to put the ten thousand in the bank to cover his losses.

"Did James' death have anything to do with the bet?" Erica was only guessing.

"Yes, ma'am," McGraw said then fell silent.

"Did the Colonel provoke James into a duel so he could kill him and not pay off the debt?"

McGraw nodded. "Thet's about the truth of it, ma'am."

"I don't suppose there's any way to make Colonel Denvers pay me the money?"

"Maybe in Kansas City or St. Louis, but not here, ma'am."

"I see. Thank you for being honest, Mr. McGraw."

"Look, ma'am, about yer money problem?"

"I'll go to the bank tomorrow for a loan."

"Well, hold off on thet, ma'am," the big ramrod said. "The boys and me, well, we ain't all thet worried about the money. We know we'll get what's comin' ta us after the summer drive."

"Are you sure, Mr. McGraw?"

McGraw turned to look at the Box R cowboys.

"Anybody agin stayin' on wif no pay fer a few months? If so, say adios right here an' now."

Several cowboys got up, gathered their gear and belongings and then walked to the door with their heads down, almost as if embarrassed.

"It's alright, I understand," Erica said as they left to saddle up and ride off.

McGraw looked around, nodded and chuckled.

"Wal, we still got seven of the best cowboys thet ever tightened a cinch an' sat a saddle, ma'am. Henry, Bradley, O'Toole, Grimes, McBride, Ogden, an' the new man, Jared. An' me, a course. We ain't goin' no place, Miss Restin!"

"Thank you for staying," Erica said. "I'm grateful."

She left and walked back towards the house. The new man, the one called Jared, had sat there quietly watching her. He was tall and very handsome. She wondered if he had a female friend. Most cowboys had one in town. She had seen him that first day when he rode in for a job. He sat tall in the saddle and was nice to look at.

Suddenly the old cook met her in the yard.

"Where are those coyotes a goin', Miss Erica?"

"They're leaving, Mr. Finley. I can't pay them right now."

"Oh, fer a minute I thought it was my cookin'," the old man chuckled, then said, "Ya can't pay 'em. huh? Well, ya don't have ta pay me, unless ya want ta, ma'am."

Erica laughed. "That's sweet of you, Mr. Finley, but I will be paying you as soon as I can. So hang on."

"I will, ma'am. I surely will."

It began to snow. Erica went into the house to think.

9.

After Erica Restin left, McGraw talked to the cowboys.

"Thet Denvers is up ta no good."

"He should have ta pay up," Tug Grimes said. "Ifn he was a man he would."

"He would ifn he had any honor but he ain't and he won't," the ramrod said. "An' there ain't nothin' anybody kin do about it."

"Hell," O'Toole said. "It was a fool's bet anyway. Neither one had thet much money to toss around."

"Yeah, I suppose so," McGraw said.

The big man got up, stretched, yawned and walked slowly towards his room in the back. He motioned for Punch Elliot and Jared to follow him.

"I gotta talk ta ya a minute, Jared."

Jared followed them in.

"Close the door and take a seat," McGraw said.

McGraw pointed to a chair near the table. Jared sat down. The ramrod took out the fixings and started to build a cigarette.

"What's up, Boss?" Jared asked.

The ramrod swiped a match against his boot heel and lit the cigarette.

"I saw how you ventilated thet bastard Merkle even when he had the drop on ya. It took guts ta do thet."

Jared shrugged. "I had to. He was about to drill Punch again."

"I won't fergit thet, Jared," Punch said. "Dutch Merkle would a done me in good an' thet's fer sure. Thanks agin." He adjusted the bandage on his shoulder.

McGraw stared at Jared "I think the Colonel is gonna make a move on the Box R."

"Because I drilled Dutch Merkle?"

McGraw nodded. "Yep! Thet and 'cause he hates the Brits."

"Hates the Restins? He hates them because they're British? How come?"

"It's got somethin' ta do with his bein' captured in the war. All I know is he hates the Brits somethin' awful."

"That's crazy."

"Crazy or not, it's a fact."

"I know a lot of people don't like them coming over here and buying up the ranches, but---" Jared stopped.

"Thet's true, Jared. But so are the tenderfoots from the east. It's all the same."

"Most cowpokes like to work for them," Jared said.

"Well, the Restins have been honest and true, an' thet's a fact."

Jared nodded in agreement. "I got no complaints."

"What I'm a getting' at is, I'm worried fer Miss Erica's safety, Jared."

"You think she's in danger?"

"I sure do," McGraw said gravely.

"From Denvers?"

"Yep. Thet's my guess."

"But why?"

"From what my sources tell me, he wants the grass and water. Thet's another reason why he plugged Mr. Restin."

Jared nodded. "Yeah. It always comes down to graze and water. Every time. I've seen this before."

"An' thet's why I want ya ta keep an eye on the lady," the ramrod said.

"Follow her around?"

"Yeah, but not so she notices. Keep outta sight, ifn ya git my drift? Kin ya do thet? At least until we settle with the Colonel."

"You think she needs protection?"

"Yep. An' it's gonna git worse afore it gits better."

"I can't believe he'd go against the code."

"After thet little trick at the Black Latigo and what he did ta Mr. Restin, ya better believe it, Jared."

Jared nodded. "Yeah. I guess I better."

"Okay, then," the ramrod said. "From now on she don't leave the yard without you bein' on her trail. Ifn she goes ta town, you best be goin' ta town too. Got it?"

Jared nodded, got up and left.

10.

The first sign of serious trouble came in January when Tug Grimes rode back from the east line shack with the bullet-ridden bodies of Red McBride and Cory Ogden tied across the saddles of their horses.

"Who did it?" McGraw growled tensely.

"I couldn't rightly tell fer sure," Grimes said.

"How come yer alive, Tug?"

"Because I winged one of 'em an' they scattered like scared hens," Grimes replied. "I winged the bastard good!"

McGraw scratched his chin in thought.

"It should be easy ta find him, then."

"Yep. He can't hide bein' shot in the arm."

"Ifn he's with the Triangle D, I'll know by tomorry," the big ramrod said. "I got friends there they don't know about." He paused to look at the bodies of his men and nodded. "Let's get 'em in outta the cold before they stiffin' up. I'll get the cook an' Jared a workin' on the boxes."

McGraw called what was left of the Box R cowboys outside and they carried the bodies of McBride and Ogden into the bunkhouse, laid them on their cots and wrapped them in their blankets. The old cook, Finley, groaned.

"Seems like I do more box makin' than cooking these days," the old man complained.

The old cook and Jared headed for the barn. Henry, Elliot, Bradley and O'Toole went behind the bunkhouse to dig the graves.

Grimes looked at McGraw. "I guess the dance has started, pard."

Stoker McGraw nodded.

"An' there's only Henry, Bradley, O'Toole, Jared, Elliot, me and you left," Grimes noted. "It ain't much, is it?"

The big ramrod nodded. "Dynamite comes in small packages, Tug."

"Yeah, it sure does," Grimes chuckled. "Ya think the Triangle D is itchin' ta dance, Stoke?"

"Well, ifn they are, we'll oblige them. I know a few fancy steps the likes of ol' Denvers ain't never seen."

They chuckled then fell silent. They had just lost two dear comrades who would never ride with them again.

"Ya gotta tell Miss Restin, Stoke," Tug Grimes said.

Stoker McGraw shrugged. "Yeah, I guess so."

"She ain't gonna like this one bit."

"I know. She don't need this kinda trouble. She's had enough already," the ramrod said.

"She sure has," Grimes opined.

"But I gotta tell her jest the same."

"Maybe we never shoulda took Dutch Merkle up on thet fight," Grimes continued. "It's what started it all."

"Yeah, but I think Denvers had it all planned out so as ta kill Restin," the ramrod said. "Anyway, it's too late now. We done what we done an' did what we did, an' we gotta make the best of it."

"What about the lady, Stoke? Does she have ta live with it, too?"

The big man clenched a fist. His face suddenly took on an intense look.

Grimes stared at McGraw, waiting for his answer.

"No, she don't. We gotta keep her safe. If Denvers lays a hand on her it'll be his last days. He'll meet his maker at the end of a rope! I swear by the code he will!"

"Amen," Grimes added.

Stoker McGraw knew he and the few cowhands left at the Box R were in a fix. Denvers had the winning hand. At least for now. As far as Denvers' ramrod Dutch Merkle was concerned, McGraw was glad the new man Jared had plugged him. If he hadn't, Punch Elliot, his best friend, would be dead.

"Well, I gotta tell Miss Restin," McGraw said. "She'll find out one way or the other. Nobody around Haverston Junction kin keep a secret. It always comes out."

With that, the ramrod left the bunkhouse and went up to the house and knocked on the door. In a few seconds Erica Restin opened it.

"Oh, Mr. McGraw! What can I do for you, sir?"

"Kin we talk, ma'am?"

As they went into her brother's study, she asked, "Was that two bodies I saw Grimes bring in, Mr. McGraw?"

"Yes, ma'am. McBride and Ogden."

"What happened?"

"They were ambushed."

"Ambushed? By whom?"

"I don't know, ma'am, but I suspect it was the Triangle D men."

"Are you sure?"

"No, ma'am. Not yet."

"But why? Is there something going on I should know about? Does it concern the Box R?"

"It does, ma'am."

"But, how?"

"You probably wouldn't understand, Miss Restin, ma'am. It about water and grass and bein' just downright mean to yer neighbors. An' takin' what ya want any way ya want because ya kin."

"I see. You're saying Colonel Denvers wants the Box R Ranch. Is that what you're saying?"

"Thet's about it, ma'am."

"I see. And you're right, I don't understand. I don't understand why there is no law here to stop that kind of thing."

"You'll have ta wait another twenty years fer thet ta come about, ma'am. Ifn yer here."

"Oh, I will be, Mr. McGraw. I will be. I will not run and I will not give in. He took my brother but he will not run me scared. I'm a Restin, Mr. McGraw, a Restin!"

Erica Restin stood tall staring at the big ramrod, looking into his eyes. He saw iron in hers.

"Thet's all I need ta know, ma'am," Stoker McGraw said. "I'll tell the boys."

"I'll attend the burial."

"No need to, ma'am."

"I want to. I have to. McBride and Ogden died for my brand, it's the least I can do. Do you have a Bible?"

"No, ma'am. I don't think so."

"I'll bring mine."

The big man nodded. Erica Restin got her shawl and followed him down behind the bunkhouse to the burial site.

Everyone stood there until Henry, Bradley, Jared and O'Toole came out of the bunkhouse carrying the coffins. They lowered them with ropes. Then they started filling in the holes. The wind made it difficult by blowing the loose dirt from the shovels before it dropped.

It took a long time to fill the holes in.

Erica read from the Psalms and when she was finished, Tonsils O'Toole sang, "Down by the Glenside." She choked back her tears as she listened, not so much from the words as from the sincere passion and force in the man's voice.

"I'm very sorry for your loss," she said and went back to the house.

When she got inside, she wept for a long time.

11.

The Slade brothers worked out of a hotel in Wichita. Their specialty was graft, protection and murder-for-hire. When times were lean, they took to rustling, but that didn't happen very often. They were originally from Ohio and had served in the Army of Ohio, in Colonel Denvers' unit. He didn't know them because they were under someone else's command, but Merkle and Malone did. During the war the Slade brothers had robbed and pillaged on the way south and even robbed a few banks. Merkle and Malone usually were in on it with them.

Mongoose Malone contacted them from time to time, just for old time's sake. Now that he was ramrod, he saw an opportunity to hire his old pals. They were fast with a gun and that was what he needed.

"I'll have one of the Slade brothers come down from Wichita, Colonel," Malone told Denvers. "He'll take care of our little problem with the Box R."

"How's he going to do that, Malone?"

"Easy. First he'll scare the hell outta thet Restin woman. Before you know it, she'll be beggin' somebody ta take the ranch off her hands."

"Is he as fast as that new man at the Box R? The one they call Jared?"

"Hell, yes! Ifn Jared sticks his nose in he'll get it shot off, thet's fer sure!"

"Then why not take him out, too? He shot Dutch, didn't he?"

"Yes, sir, he sure did, the rotten son of a bitch!"

The Colonel pondered the consequences of getting rid of the woman and the cowboy all at once, without being implicated. So far he was respected in the area. He was active in the town's activities. He even got the old marshal elected to office, as well as most of the town council.

"How much for Jared and the woman?" the Colonel asked.

Malone's small brain raced and searched for a convincing figure. "Fifteen hundred?"

"Can he come in here, do the job and leave in one day?"

"Oh, sure, no problem with thet, Colonel."

"But fifteen is a bit too high," the Colonel said.

"He has ta come all the way from Wichita, Colonel. I don't think he'll come fer less than fifteen."

The Colonel sighed. "Alright, fifteen, then. But don't bring him around me or the ranch. I don't even want to see his face."

"About thet woman? How far do ya want him ta go with her?"

"I don't care one way or the other as long as I get first bid on the Box R."

That same day Malone rode into town and sent a wire to the Monarch Hotel in Wichita addressed to R. Slade. It read:

"Old pal. A one-day job. One thousand. Meet me at the Black Latigo Saloon in Haverston Junction on next Monday at five. Signed, Malone."

Mongoose Malone figured he'd take five hundred off the top as a finder's fee. After all, he was doing all the setting up and footwork.

That coming Monday, Malone and Slade met at the Black Latigo Saloon. They shook hands and slapped backs.

"Dang," Malone said. "It's good ta see ya, Ringo. How's Norm, Tally an' Ed?"

"Jest great, Goose!" Slade chuckled, using the shorter version of Malone's nickname. "Jest Great. Damn ifn we don't miss the war an all!"

"Yeah. It sure was easy pickin's. I'm working fer the Colonel now."

"Where's Dutch?"

"Thet's why I sent fer ya, Ringo. Dutch was bush-wacked by a Box R cowboy named Jared."

"How come you ain't braced him, Goose? In the old days you'd a braced the bastard!"

"The Colonel don't want me ta start a war," Malone said. "Thet's why he's a paying you top money ta do the job. He don't want the Triangle D ta be connected."

"So he wants me ta brace this Jared?"

"Yeah, but there's somethin' else."

"What's thet?"

"He wants ta buy the Box R Ranch where this Jared works. It's owned by a woman. She won't sell."

Ringo Slade chuckled. "I see. Where do I find her an' him?"

"He's been a followin' her like a love sick puppy fer the past week. She comes ta town regular like, to Brinkston's Mercantile. He sorta stays back in the shadows watchin' out fer her."

Slade chuckled. "Poor sap."

Malone went on, "An' the Colonel don't care ifn she gits in the way when ya brace him. Ya git my drift?"

"I sure do, Goose," Slade said. "This should be a real hoot and a holler, Goose."

Ringo Slade was very confident.

12.

Clay Jared followed Erica Restin into Haverston Junction. He stopped to tie his horse in front of a beanery while she continued further down the road to Brinkston's Mercantile. The cowboy was pretending to tighten his cinch when she came up to him.

"You're not doing a very good job of spying on me, Mr. Jared."

Jared, caught off guard, gave a start then chuckled.

"I snuck up on you, didn't I?" she said, smiling.

"You sure did, ma'am," the cowboy replied.

He had trailed her as she rode the buckboard all the way from the ranch into town to do some shopping.

"I've been on to you all along, Mr. Jared. You're not very good at snooping."

She saw him that first time from her library window as he rode tall and straight in the saddle. He looked just like the pictures in the penny dreadful magazines she used to secretly read back in London. Her mother and father never knew she had a pile under her bed.

This new cowboy was handsome but also had a rough edge, and there was something unique about him the others lacked. It was obvious he came from good stock. You could see it in the way he carried himself, the way he walked. He held his head up and kept his eyes straight ahead, confident but not boastful.

She heard the other cowboys talking about how Jared had faced Dutch Merkle even though Merkle had the drop on him, all to save the life of Punch Elliot. He had lived up to her expectations of what a real cowboy was. It pleased and amused her when Jared first started following her. Now it made her feel special.

"Please don't tell Stoker McGraw you found me out, ma'am," Jared kidded. "I'll get laughed plumb off the Box R Ranch."

"Rest assured, Mr. Jared," Erica chuckled. "It'll be our little secret." She stared up at him. "I'll be in Mr. Brinkston's store for a while. I'll be perfectly safe there, so you can relax."

"Yes, ma'am," Jared said, thinking how beautiful and refined she was. Even her voice was beautiful. "I'll go over to see the marshal and talk a while."

Jared tipped his hat as she walked away towards the mercantile. He waited until she had gone in and walked up the road to the jailhouse.

Marshal Tolliver was an old, silver-haired man who walked with a limp from being shot in his left leg. He had a shaggy white mustache that hid his upper lip and dropped down the sides of his face. He was small and frail. The marshal's badge seemed large enough and heavy enough to weigh him down.

He was alone when Jared walked into his jail.

"What kin I do fer ya, bub?" Marshal Tolliver asked.

"Hi, Marshal. My name's Clay Jared. I work for the Box R."

The Marshal squinted at Jared, trying to remember where he had seen him before.

"The Box R, ya say?"

"Yes. The Restin spread."

"Well, whatta ya want, Jared?"

"There's gonna be a war between the Box R and the Triangle D."

The marshal chuckled. "A war, ya say?" He scratched his chin. "We ain't had one of them in years. Not since the Circle N had it out with the Flyin' T. We had ta call the Army in."

"People are going to die unless someone steps in to stop it, Marshal."

"Well, the Colonel is the man ta do thet," the marshal said. "He's got all the pull around here. Yep. The Colonel is the man ta talk to, Jabob."

"Jared."

"What's thet?"

"My name's Jared, not Jabob, Marshal." Jared looked around the jail. It wasn't much to see, just one cell, a desk and a gun rack with a Winchester and a scattergun.

"How many deputies do you have, Marshal?"

"One and I'm lucky ta have him. This one-horse town can't afford but one."

"I see," Jared said. He suddenly noticed what appeared to be a man on the floor of the cell.

"Is he dead, Marshal?"

The marshal laughed. "Hell no. Thet's Henry Hunter, the town drunk!"

Suddenly Jared realized what a dire situation Erica Restin was in. It all boiled down to the Colonel, and, like the marshal said, he was king in Haverston Junction. That did not bode well for her or the Box R. There was very little law in Haverston Junction.

Jared nodded to the marshal and left, walking back down the street to where his horse and the buckboard were tied. He stood there watching the door of the mercantile. While it was only thirty feet away it seemed a long way off.

After a while Erica Restin came out with an armful of packages. She put them in the back of the buckboard. As she did so, a man came across the street from the Half Moon Saloon.

He was medium tall and wore tight black leather clothing. His black hat, boots and vest were adorned with Mexican conchas. A blue bandana hung loosely around his neck, setting off his pale skin. He wore his hat tilted back, showing his smile. He had soft blue eyes set in a refined looking face. Everything about him said killer.

The man swaggered confidently up to Erica Restin.

"Good day, Miss Restin," he said, touching the brim of his hat in a salute. "It sure is a fine day for this early in the year, wouldn't you say?"

Erica stared at the man, sizing him up.

"Do I know you, sir?"

"No, but we have a mutual friend," the man said. He glanced down the road at Clay Jared and nodded to show he saw him.

"Oh? Who might that be, sir?"

"Colonel Denvers, ma'am."

"He's no friend of mine, sir," the woman said bluntly.

The man chuckled "Well, I could be your friend, Miss Restin, if you'd let me."

He put his left hand on her shoulder. Erica flinched, pulled back and brushed it away.

"The Colonel said you needed attention, Miss Restin, you being an old maid and all. He said I should take care of you, if you know what I mean."

"I know perfectly well what you mean, sir."

Slade chuckled. "How about I escort you around town?"

"I have an escort, sir."

"Oh, where?" The man pretended to look around. "I don't see any escort, ma'am."

"Over here!" Jared said loudly. He stepped into the street, away from his horse.

The gunslinger nodded and smiled. "Are you the one called Clay Jared?"

"Yeah. That's me. Who the hell are you?"

"Slade. Ringo Slade."

"Well, take a walk, Mr. Slade."

Slade took a step away from Erica Restin and took up the stance.

"Make me!" Slade growled.

He reached for Erica with his left hand, grabbing her arm, trying to pull her into the line of fire as he drew with his right hand. She pulled back.

Both men drew at the same time. Slade tried for a head shot. His bullet sent Jared's hat spinning in the air. Jared, in a low crouch, fanned off a quick shot, hitting Slade in the belly. Just to make sure, he fanned off two more shots into the gunslinger's chest. Slade did a little dance before collapsing in a heap.

Erica Restin screamed and turned away, gasping in horror.

She had heard the thud of bullets as they slammed into Slade's body. He was so close his blood splattered on her arm and dress. Now he lay dead on the road at her very feet.

Jared holstered his Colt and ran to catch Erica as she fainted. People quickly gathered around them. He rushed through the crowd, up the porch and into the mercantile, setting her on a chair. They followed him.

"Is she hurt?" Herb Brinkston, the owner, asked. His wife saw Erica and quickly got her a glass of water.

"Oh, dear, shame on me," Erica said as she came around. "Did I faint?"

"Sort of," Jared said, rubbing the circulation back into her hands. He untied his bandana and wiped the blood off her right arm.

Marshal Tolliver came limping into the store carrying Jared's hat. He looked around, spotted Jared and walked over to him and Erica.

"They said you potted thet buzzard out there."

"He braced me," Jared said.

The marshal chuckled and held up the hat. He stuck his finger in a bullet hole in the left side of the crown.

"You were lucky, sonny. Another inch ta tha right an' you'd a been pushin' up daisies. An' thet's fer sure!" He tossed the hat to Jared. "But ya owe tha town five double eagles, my friend."

"How come?"

"Casket and burial."

"His horse and saddle should more than cover it," Jared said. "And check his pockets. He looks like he'd have plenty."

The marshal thought that over and nodded.

"Fair enough," He looked at Erica Restin. "What happened, Miss Restin?"

"That man out there assaulted me, Marshal Tolliver, and Mr. Jared came to my rescue."

"Then he got what was a comin' to him," the marshal said. "Do you need a doctor, ma'am?"

"No. I'm alright."

The marshal left. Erica looked at Jared.

"Would you please take me home, Mr. Jared?" Erica said.

Jared nodded and left. He got his horse and tied it to the buckboard. Erica was waiting in front. He helped her up on the seat then got up next to her and they drove off.

At first they didn't talk, but a few miles out of town he spoke. "If I might ask, ma'am, why did you and your brother leave England?"

"James was always the overprotective brother. I married badly, lost a child, went into depression, then had a divorce. He suggested we should come here to heal."

"Then you didn't intend to stay forever?"

"No, just a few years. James was always the adventurous one. The wild frontier and all that. And I suppose I had romantic notions about the American West, too. I'd read a lot of romantic stories about it."

"Then you're going to sell the ranch now that your brother is---"

"Dead? I haven't decided yet. This world of yours scares me but there is something exhilarating about it, as savage as it is. Strangely, it appeals to me. It's full of surprises. Like today."

Jared chuckled. "Yeah. Like today."

"If your aim had been off by an inch I might be dead now," she said.

"He tried to get you in the line of fire. I had to act fast," Jared said. "I'm sorry."

"Don't be sorry. Someday I'll tell the story to my children and grandchildren," Erica chuckled. "I'll tell how I almost, as you cowboys say, bought the farm or cashed in my chips."

Jared laughed. "You're learning to speak cowboy, ma'am."

"Yes, I guess I am," she said, smiling.

She leaned against him, her head on his shoulder, her hands gripping his arm. He could feel her heart beating. She was still scared.

"Do you mind? I feel a little done in, Mr. Jared."

"Please. It's my pleasure, ma'am."

Jared slowed the pace of the horse to make the buckboard ride gentle. She held his arm tight as if afraid he would pull away.

He had no intention of doing that.

13.

Stoker McGraw knew what was going on. His informant in the Colonel's camp told him everything.

"Denvers is goin' fer the throat, men," McGraw told his cowboys as they sat around him in the bunkhouse one bleak evening. "Yesterday his hired gunslinger, Ringo Slade, made a move on Miss Restin."

"Thet ain't right," Pages Henry said.

"An' it's dead agin the code," Tonsil O'Toole said.

"It sure is," Tug Grimes added. "An' we can't let it stand."

"It didn't. Jared put three lead pills in Slade's belly, an' done it neat an' clean."

"Except fer Jared's hat a gettin' in the way," Charcoal Bradley chuckled. "Now he's got an extra air hole in it!"

They all chuckled.

"But thet ain't the end of it," the big ramrod explained. "As I hear it, there's more ta come."

"How's thet?" Henry asked.

"Ringo Slade has three little brothers over in Wichita," McGraw said. "They're a coming this way ta finish off Jared and the miss."

There was a deep silence as the full meaning of McGraw's words set in.

"And the Colonel is the one behind it all," McGraw added, "in case ya hadn't guessed."

O'Toole whistled.

"I guess we got us a war," Grimes said.

"I said it was a comin' and now it is," the ramrod said solemnly. "We didn't ask the Colonel fer this, but he's a forcin' it on us. He's lookin' ta see if we'll high tail it an' run."

"This ain't good," Bradley said. "More people are gonna die, Stoke."

"Well, ifn anybody wants ta take off fer higher ground, good riddance ta ya. Ya kin sneak outta here ta night. But ya best move fast an' not let me ketch ya."

"What about the marshal?" Henry asked. "Maybe he can talk to the Colonel. Stop it before it starts."

"It's already started," McGraw said.

"I already talked to the marshal," Jared said. "He's an old man with a bad leg and only a part-time deputy. And he's afraid of Denvers."

"So much for the law," Punch Elliot chuckled.

"The law can't help us none, anyway," McGraw said. "Denvers is slick. He's gonna wipe us out and make it look like self-defense. Hell, those of us he don't kill he'll have hung as rustlers!"

"Christ! Ya tryin' ta scared us, Stoke?" O'Toole asked.

"Thet's exactly what I'm tryin' ta do," McGraw growled. "I don't want no yella-bellies alongside me when this thing explodes. I want a man ready ta kill fer the brand. If thet ain't you then hit the trail an' adios, you faint-hearted son of a bitch!"

No one spoke for a while.

"What's the Colonel really want, Stoke?" Bradley asked.

"He wants the Box R, is what he wants. He wants it like a honey bear wants honey an' a lush wants whiskey. He wants the Box R water and graze an' he's gonna kill ta git it."

Again, there was an uneasy silence. Suddenly McGraw went into his room. Punch Elliot and Grimes followed.

Pages Henry got out his volume of *Moby Dick* and looked at the pictures for the thousandth time. Charcoal Bradley opened his sketch pad and starting drawing something. Tonsils O'Toole broke out a deck of cards and started to play solitaire, singing low to himself. They all could hear the horses down in the corral snorting and stomping about as if they sensed death coming.

Clay Jared thought about Erica Restin being all alone in the big house. It was getting dark out. He got up from his bunk, grabbed a blanket and started for the door.

"Where ya goin'?" O'Toole asked.

"I'm gonna keep an eye on the house, jest in case," Jared said.

O'Toole nodded. "Give a holler if ya need backup."

"Sure."

Jared left, walked up to the porch and sat in a chair with his blanket wrapped around him.

"Is that you, Mr. Jared?"

"Yes, ma'am."

Erica Restin came out of the house with a heavy wool shawl around her shoulders.

"It's going to be a cold night, Mr. Jared."

He could see the wind playing in her hair whipping it about, tugging at it. She looked up at the fading sky.

"It's very lovely here," she said.

"Yes."

"Are you intending to stay out here long?"

"Yes. All night."

"The couch would be better," she whispered.

"Are you sure, ma'am?"

"Yes, I'm sure."

"Alright."

They went into the house.

Some time during the night she came down from her bedroom, crawled under the blanket and lay next to him on the couch. She was shivering from the cold.

"Do you mind, Mr. Jared?"

"No, ma'am."

They huddled, listening to the winter wind whining across the yard outside and the coyotes howling in the hills behind the barn.

14.

Things had not turned out the way that Mongoose Malone had promised. Colonel Denvers was very upset. Malone was standing before him in his study.

"What happened, Mr. Malone? What went wrong?"

"That son of a bitch, Jared, got lucky. The woman must have distracted Slade just as he drew. I'm sure that's what happened."

"And where's my fifteen hundred dollars now, Mr. Malone?"

"Ah, well Colonel, I guess it's still in Slade's pocket, most likely."

"And if the marshal finds it he'll know why Slade came here, Mr. Malone. He'll add things up."

"Hell, that old fart? He ain't gonna do nothin'. He'll just take the money. He's as crooked as a snake, the old bastard," Malone said, trying to make light of it.

He let out with a nervous laugh.

The Colonel did not see the humor at all. He gave Malone a hard, penetrating stare that caused the little man to shrink back.

"Mr. Malone, I paid to have a job done and I want it done. This was your idea, so fix it. I don't care how you fix it but just do it. Do it or you're finished here at the Triangle D. Is that plain enough, Mr. Malone?"

"Yes, sir!"

"Good! Now get out of my sight!"

Mongoose Malone left, slinked down to the bunkhouse and sat in the back room thinking about his situation, which was not good. After an hour of trying to figure things out, he walked down to the corral, saddled up his horse and rode into town. Going directly to the train depot he sent a wire to Norman Slade at the Monarch Hotel in Wichita. It read:

"Ringo ambushed by Box R cowboys. Signed, M. Malone."

After sending the wire, Malone rode slowly back to the Triangle D. Soon the Slade brothers would come to avenge their older brother, Ringo. Now all he had to do was to get them to brace the Box R cowhands and put an end to it.

If everything worked out as planned, the Restin woman would sell out and the Colonel could get first bid. He had a pull with the bank, and no one else around would bid against him. When the dust cleared, Denvers would own the Box R and Malone would be back in the Colonel's good graces.

He'd prove that he was as good as Dutch.

15.

When Norman Slade got the wire saying his older brother Ringo had been killed by Box R cowboys, he got very, very angry. Added to that was the fact that things were not going all that well for the Slade brothers in Wichita.

A new marshal had been appointed by the city council and he was nobody's fool. He was sharp and smart and was cracking down on the graft and corruption in that notorious city. His two deputies, both once Texas Rangers, were just as mean.

"Hell, Norm," Tally Slade said, "let's git the heck outta here. This town is a gettin' too darned civilized, if ya ask me."

"Where the hell you think we should go?" Norm Slade asked. "Dodge City is even worse.

"Maybe we could hang around Haverston Junction with Malone," Ed, the youngest of the brothers said. "Since we're gonna be there ta settle up with those sidewinders that kilt Ringo."

Norm Slade let that percolate in his mind a moment.

"Yeah, we could do thet. Maybe thet Colonel who Malone is workin' fer kin use our kinda services. It looks like it ta me."

Tally and Ed Slade nodded in agreement. From the wire that Malone had sent, it looked like the Colonel could use some persuaders like them to settle his Box R problem. Also they were still stung by the death of their oldest brother, Ringo. He was the lynchpin of the group. They would bring retribution down on the Box R cowboys for killing him.

They left Wichita and headed south towards Caldwell, then rode west towards Haverston Junction. They were there four days later and sitting in the Black Latigo Saloon. They were in a bad mood as the cold wind had dogged them all the way. It was a bad trip. They perked up a little when Mongoose Malone came to greet them.

"Good ta see ya, Goose!" Norm Slade said.

"The drinks are on me, men," Malone said.

They took a table and ordered food and drinks. After a few rounds of rotgut, they got down to business. The Slade brothers were anxious to get things moving.

"Where do we find these Box R boys?" Tally asked. "I'm anxious ta drill their asses."

"And you will," Malone said. "An' I'll be right with ya all the way, Tally. All the way!"

"Where's Ringo's horse an' gear?" Norm asked. "He paid four hundred jest fer thet fancy saddle. Had it special made."

"An' them twin Colts and belt put him back a few hundred," Ed, the young one said. "I think he said three hundred."

"Six hundred," Norm said. "More like six hundred. An' countin' the horse and saddlebags, yer lookin' at a thousand bucks."

"He also had the thousand you paid him, right, Goose?" Tally asked. Malone nodded.

"So, where's it all at?" Norm asked coldly.

Malone shrugged. "You'll have to see the marshal about that, men. He's got it all, as far I know."

"Where's Ringo buried?" Tally asked.

Over in the Haverston Junction graveyard," Malone said. "I suspect that since Ringo had all that money and fancy outfit, the marshal gave him a right fancy burial. That's usually how it works out."

"Well, jest maybe we'll give the marshal a fancy burial. An' those Box R boys too," Norm hissed.

"Give us some names, Goose," Tally said. "I want their goddam names! The ones thet kilt Ringo!"

Malone nodded and took a drink, thinking as he did. This was the chance to get rid of the top men at the Box R. Once they were cut down, the rest would run like scared rabbits.

"Tug Grimes, Clay Jared and the ramrod, Stoker McGraw," Malone lied. "They were the three who did it."

"I wanna brace 'em all," Tally growled. "I want ta kill them bastards so bad I kin taste it!"

"Not alone," Norm Slade said. "I want a piece of the action, too, Tal." He looked over at his younger brother. "Ed, this is yer chance ta show yer grit. We're gonna meet them three sidewinders face ta face and ventilate 'em all."

Ed Slade nodded. He wasn't all that eager to face down anybody in a shootout. He wasn't all that fast on the draw. Also, he had a girlfriend back in Wichita. A pretty one.

"Sure, Norm, whatever you say," the young man muttered.

"You pull this off and they'll be more work just like it," Malone said. "Once the Colonel sees how easy it is, he'll take an interest in seeing more of it. I got the feeling he wants more than just this one ranch."

"Sounds good to me," Norm Slade said. "It'll be jest like old times, Goose, when we was a burnin' and a pillagin' down south."

"Yeah," Malone said. "Those were the good old days."

"They sure were," Tally Slade said. He turned to his younger brother and slapped him on the back. "You shoulda been there, little brother. You missed some great times."

"You sure did, Ed," Norm said. "You sure did. Didn't he, Goose?"

Malone chuckled. "Oh, yeah. Those were great times."

They fell quiet for a while, eating their stew. Finally, young Ed looked up.

"What's the law situation here, Goose?"

"Just a broke-down old marshal and one deputy."

"Didn't we pass a bank on the way here through town?" Ed continued.

"The Cattlemen's Bank? Yeah, why?"

"Much in it?"

"Yeah, it's usually loaded. You wanna make a deposit?"

"More like a withdrawal," Ed said. They all laughed except Malone.

"Whatta ya mean, Ed?"

"Well, I was thinkin' maybe we should fergit about the Box R and jest pop the bank and run.

"Then what?"

"Head south ta Blackwell, Texas, across the Red River. I heard about a hideout there where the law ain't welcome. Not even the Rangers."

Suddenly Norm glared at his younger brother.

"Yer jest yellah, aincha, Ed? Yer afraid ta do what ya gotta do. Well, yer gonna brace them polecats alongside us and like it. So buck up an' get some grit!"

Ed Slade shrunk in on himself and nodded in defeat. His attempt to save his life had failed.

"Where we gonna do it?" Tally asked.

"Right here, out in front of the Black Latigo," Malone said. "Just say when."

"The quicker the better," Norm said. "How about tomorrow at noon?"

"Alright," Malone replied. "You want me to back you all up?"

"Nope, this is a family thing," Tally said.

Mongoose Malone heaved a sigh of relief. "Sure, sure, I understand. A family thing."

Norm Slade got up from the table and stretched and yawned. "We'll go inta town and get a room fer the night. Maybe we'll look the town over."

"Any good lookers around?" Tally asked.

"Over at the Half Moon Saloon," Malone said. "Sadie Newman is a good looker."

Tally chuckled. "Sadie Newman, here I come!"

After the Slade brothers left, Mongoose Malone sat at the table drinking and thinking. He chuckled. The Slade brothers would kill Jared for him. They would avenge Dutch

Merkle's death and he wouldn't have to lift a finger or fire a shot. The Colonel would end up with the Box R and he, Malone, would be the ramrod of the biggest ranch in the area.

With the Slade brothers working for the Triangle D there was no stopping the Colonel from taking over the entire valley. They would spread fear throughout the Junction and there was no law to stop them.

Suddenly Malone felt very good about life. He left the Black Latigo and rode west towards the Triangle D. Halfway there he veered northwest towards the Box R. He got there just before sunset and rode over to the bunkhouse. He didn't dismount.

Tonsils O'Toole saw him from a window and called back to Stoker McGraw. In a moment the big ramrod rushed outside to confront the Triangle D man.

"What the hell do you want, Malone?"

"I just came from the Black Latigo, McGraw. The three Slade brothers were there. They said to tell you they want to meet you, Grimes and Jared at noon. Right there in front of the Latigo."

"You dirty skunk! You set this up, didn't ya?"

"Who, me? Why would I do a thing like that, Stoke?" Malone chuckled.

"Because yer a crooked son of a bitch, Goose, thet's why."

"Well, I just came to deliver the message. You gonna show up or run?"

"Oh, we'll be there, you rat-faced bastard!"

"In case you get past them, Stoke, come and look me up."

"Is thet a threat, Malone?"

"Take it any way you want, Stoke," Malone said.

He sent his horse galloping away.

16.

Mongoose Malone was sitting at a table in back of the Black Latigo Saloon with the Slade brothers. They were waiting for the Box R cowboys. He tied his horse to a tree out back just in case something went wrong.

"Watch out for Jared," Malone cautioned them. "He's the fast one."

"Which one is he?" Tally asked.

"He'll be the tallest of the three. And the youngest. Stoker McGraw is the old heavy one. Grimes is the shortest."

"Why don't you take Jared, Norm?" Tally said.

"What's the matter, Tally, you scared of him?"

"Hell no," Tally said. "Heck, you an' Ed kin sit here an' drink rotgut an' I'll go out there and take all three of 'em on by myself, ifn ya want."

Norm chuckled. "Sure ya would, Tal, sure ya would."

"I ain't seen no cowpoke what kin shoot worth a damn anyway," Tally said.

"Yeah, well, thet kinda stupid thinkin' will get ya pushin' up daisies, brother," Norm said.

"Screw you, Norm," Tally yelled, jumping up from the table. "Hell, I'll jest ride outta here and you and Ed kin have it all to yerselfs!"

"Calm down," Ed Slade said as he grabbed Tally's arm. "This ain't no time ta get riled up, Tal!"

"Well, tell Norm ta stop a pickin' on me, then," Tally Slade whined.

Malone looked on. It suddenly didn't look like a sure thing. The Slade brothers were starting to crack under the strain. He had to stop that.

"Look," Malone said. "As far as that Jared fellah goes, Ringo got distracted by the Restin woman. If it wasn't for her, he'd have plugged Jared fair and square. He ain't that fast."

"Ya think so, Goose?" Tally asked.

"Hell, I know so! You three can outdraw Jared and all the rest of those Box R slowpokes by a mile. Have a drink and relax," Malone said.

Norm Slade nodded.

"After I ventilate Jared, I'll do the same fer her," Norm said.

Malone refilled their shot glasses and they all took a long slug. He refilled them again.

"Let's toast," Malone said. "To Ringo. And damn the Box R cowpokes all to hell!"

"Amen!" Tally shouted and tossed his drink down in one gulp. "Sorry fer getting' all huffed up, Norm," Tally said.

"It's okay, Tal," Norm replied.

The lookout came in, nodded at them and went to the bar.

"They're here," Malone said.

The Slade brothers looked at each other.

Outside, the Box R men dismounted. They tied their horses in a stand of pine trees near the saloon, out of the line of fire, and stood in the road waiting. Jared was in the middle with McGraw to his right and Grimes to his left.

"They'll be three of 'em," Stoker McGraw said.

"What if there's more?" Grimes asked.

A light powdery snow began to fall.

"Then run like a stuck pig," McGraw said, "because it'll be an ambush comin' at ya."

Jared chuckled.

"What's so funny, Jared," Grimes asked.

"This reminds me of a little shindig I had a year ago, only it was me and a kid against four shooters."

"How'd thet pan out?" McGraw asked.

"Me and the kid both got winged but we got the job done."

"Yer a cold blooded bastard, Jared," McGraw said. "An right now I'm sure glad ya are, friend."

They stopped talking and watched three men walk out of the Black Latigo Saloon and step onto the road, staring in their direction.

"Christ!" McGraw said. "They're all dressed in black! They're damned professional gunslingers!"

Jared chuckled. "So was the one I plugged, and I suspect he was the fastest they had."

Norm Slade stood in the middle, with Tally to his right and Ed to his left. He stared up the road and called out.

"Which one of you fools is named Jared?"

"I'm facing you, mister," Jared called back. "Why?"

"Because yer the one I want. You killed my brother Ringo an' I'm gonna do the same ta you, ya no good son of a bitch."

"He was molesting a woman," Jared called back. "We kill men here for doing that."

"She musta been somethin' special," Tally Slade chuckled.

"She is. She's my boss."

"You work fer a woman?" Norm shouted back.

"Yeah, we all do," Stoker McGraw said aloud. "What's it to ya?"

"Nothin', except when we're finished with you three buzzards we'll go pay her a visit she won't ferget for a long time."

"No, you won't," Jared said.

"Why not?" Norm sneered.

"Because you'll be dead," McGraw yelled. "You'll all be eatin' dirt!"

"Draw!" they all yelled. It echoed in the cold winter air but was quickly lost in the loud bark of gunfire.

Norm and Jared, facing each other, both went into a crouch and fired. Norm Slade was a second quicker but shot too high, creasing the cowboy along the top of his left shoulder. Jared picked a spot and fanned one shot into Norm's chest and another into his stomach. The first shot froze Slade and the second one knocked him back on his heels and flat on his back.

McGraw took a bullet from Tally that tore a small chunk of flesh out of his left thigh. The big man grunted and fanned off three shots. One hit Tally in the right hip, dropping him on his knees. McGraw put one in his heart and one between his eyes. Tally Slade fell face down in the road.

Grimes fared better. The youngest Slade, Ed, threw down his gun and put his hands up.

"Adios, kid!" Grimes yelled. Ed Slade ran for his horse and rode off. Grimes holstered his gun. "Shit. You guys had all the fun."

Jared and McGraw were busy reloading their Colts.

"Are you hit bad, Boss?" Jared asked the big ramrod.

"Not so much," McGraw said, wrapping his bandana around his left leg. "Now, let's go finish this thing."

McGraw limped down the road and went into the Black Latigo Saloon and stood in the doorway. Jared and Grimes lined up beside him. They took up the stance.

"Any Triangle D men here?" McGraw bellowed.

"Yeah," someone yelled back. "But this ain't our dance. It's Goose Malone yer lookin' fer, McGraw."

"Where is the dirty sidewinder?"

"The ugly bastard jest lit out like a scalded skunk," someone chuckled.

McGraw went up to the bar.

"Three rotguts, Barney," he said as if nothing had happened and he had just dropped in for a drink.

"Sure thing, Stoke!"

Jared and Grimes stepped up beside McGraw. They drank, had a second, paid and left.

They went outside, stripped the gun belts off the Slade brothers, stuffed them in their saddlebags and tied the bodies over the saddles. They headed for Haverston Junction with the horses in tow. When they got there they stopped at the marshal's office.

"What the hell's all this?" the marshal groaned. "More bodies? What the hell is a goin' on, McGraw?"

"It's a long story," McGraw said. "Ya got time ta listen?"

"Hell, I got all night!" Marshal Tolliver looked at the bodies. "This should be a real good one, Stoke."

"Oh, it is," Grimes said.

They went inside. McGraw told the story of how Colonel Denvers, Dutch Merkle and Mongoose Malone conspired to take control of the Box R, using the Slade brothers.

"Bring me some proof," the old man said. "I'll need it."

The left and rode back to the Box R. Erica Restin met them as they rode in. When she saw that Jared and the ramrod had been shot, she made them sit in the kitchen.

"It ain't all thet serious, ma'am," McGraw said.

Erica got out the medicine box and cut his pant leg to get at the wound. After cleaning it she wrapped a clean bandage around it. She did the same for Jared.

"You were lucky, Mr. McGraw," she said. "I'll change the bandage again, tomorrow. You, too, Mr. Jared."

"Thank you, ma'am," he said.

McGraw got up, saluted, left the house and limped down to the bunkhouse. As Jared started to leave, Erica stopped him.

"Is it all over now?" she asked.

"Almost, ma'am," Jared said.

"There's more?"

"A little more."

She put a hand on his cheek and kissed him lightly on the mouth.

"Thank you for standing up for me, Mr. Jared," she said softly, looking into his eyes.

Jared chuckled. "Ma'am, please don't kiss me like that again."

"Why? Don't you like it?"

"Oh, I like it alright," Jared said. "That's just the problem."

He looked a little overwhelmed.

She smiled. "I see. Alright then, I'll not kiss you unless you tell me to. Is that fair?"

"Yes, ma'am."

Jared left and walked slowly down to the bunkhouse feeling conflicted. He hadn't expected the kiss.

"What's the matter, Jared?" McGraw said. "Ya look like ya been thrown by a wild bronc!"

"Or been kissed by a pretty woman," O'Toole said.

Jared turned away and went to his bunk. He came close to blushing.

17.

It was late Friday night and Mongoose Malone had just wrapped up a wild night at the Black Latigo Saloon. He said his goodbyes, went outside to urinate, mounted his horse and rode away toward the Triangle D with a bottle of rotgut in his hand.

As he rode along he thought about the Colonel. Nothing had worked out as he promised the Colonel it would. The Colonel was very mad about that and demanded Malone put things right. Malone had no idea how he was going to do that. What with Dutch Merkle and the Slade brothers gone, he was all alone. Maybe it was time to move on. Go back to Ohio.

When he came to a place where the road cut through a stand of tall pine trees he was suddenly jerked from the saddle. Someone slammed him alongside the head with a gun butt and knocked him cold.

Malone came to in the Haverston Junction jail house. He was sitting in a chair next to the marshal's desk. He noticed a burlap bag on it but gave it no mind.

His head hurt and his mouth was sand dry. He looked around and saw the marshal, Stoker McGraw, Tug Grimes and Clay Jared.

"What's going on, Marshal?" Malone asked. "Why am I here? Have I done somethin'?"

"Well, thets what we're gonna figure out, Malone," Marshal Tolliver said. "There's been some serious charges agin ya."

"Who by, Marshal?"

"By me," McGraw said.

Malone chuckled, then groaned, holding his throbbing head. Finally, he said, "What charges, McGraw?"

"Thet Dutch Merkle an' you consorted wif Colonel Denvers ta kill Miss Restin an' git holt of the Box R."

"Why would we do thet?"

"We're a wastin' time," Grimes growled. "Stick his hand in the damn sack."

Malone's eyes fastened onto the burlap sack on the marshal's desk. Its mouth was tied shut.

"What's in the sack?" Malone asked, his voice breaking.

It suddenly moved as if alive.

"A diamond back rattler," McGraw said. "An he's mad as hell."

"You wouldn't---"

"Put yer hand in there? Hell yes."

"Give me a deal," Malone said.

"Sure," the ramrod chuckled. "You confess an' we won't put yer hand in the sack."

"How about I spill the beans on the Colonel and ride on. I ain't been to Ohio in a while."

"Okay," McGraw said. "I'll go along with thet." He turned to the marshal. "Is thet good enough, Tom?"

"Sure," the marshal said. "Thet's fine with me. Spill it an' get the hell outta my town, Malone."

Jared wrote down Malone's statement. He read it back to the marshal. The old lawman nodded. Malone signed it.

"Malone," McGraw said. "If I see ya around here after tonight. I'll drill ya. Ifn I don't, Grimes or Jared will."

Malone rushed outside, mounted up and rode away into the night.

The marshal chuckled. "Ya kin take thet bag outside an' let the rat loose now, Grimes."

After Malone left, McGraw cornered the marshal.

"Tom, where's thet thousand dollars Ringo Slade had on him when Jared plugged him? You ain't stole it, have ya?"

"You know me better than thet, Stoke. It's right there in the safe. But I had ta sell his horse, guns and gear fer the burial."

"I guess ya made a little offn thet, Tom."

"Some. God knows I don't git paid all thet much by the town.

"Well, thet thousand belongs ta Jared," the ramrod said. "As fer the other gear from Norm and Tally, I don't care what ya do with it. It's all yours."

The old marshal nodded. "Fair enough, Stoke, fair enough."

The marshal opened the safe and handed the money to Jared who put it in his shirt pocket. "Thanks, Marshal."

"Don't spend it all in one place, sonny." The marshal chuckled. "An don't try yer luck over at the Half Moon. It's crooked."

"This money is going to the Box R," Jared said. "To get it through to the next drive to Ellsworth."

McGraw chuckled. "She got under yer skin, didn't she, Jared?"

Jared shrugged. "A little, I guess."

The marshal turned to McGraw.

"What's yer next move, Stoke?"

"The Colonel," Stoker McGraw said. "It's his turn ta pay the piper, Tom. He's been gittin' his way fer too long now.

"Whose gonna make him pay, Stoke? You?"

"Maybe."

The marshal laughed. "Thet's a pretty big job, Stoke. He's broke everybody who tried it. No, you ain't gonna git no satisfaction outta the Colonel. There ain't enough law out here jest yet ta do thet."

The big ramrod stroked his bristly chin, looking thoughtful. "Well, he's gotta pay somehow fer murderin' my boss."

"It was a duel, fair an' square," the marshal said. "No jury out here will convict him of murderin' Restin."

"Restin never fired a gun in his life 'ceptin' a shotgun, and Denvers knew thet."

The marshal shrugged.

"Well, lookin' at it theta way, I guess ya could call it murder."

"What would you call it, Tom?"

The marshal nodded in agreement.

"Murder, I guess. But, like I said, there ain't enough law out here yet ta do anything about it."

McGraw chuckled. "There's more than one kinda law, Tom. Remember how we did it in the old days?"

"I never heard ya say thet, Stoke," the marshal said seriously. "Ya never said thet to me. Now get the hell outta my jail!"

The big ramrod chuckled.

"Sure, Marshal, whatever ya say."

Stoker McGraw laughed hard as he left the jail house.

McGraw, Grimes and Jared left and rode slowly back to the Box R.

"Thet thousand dollars? You really givin' it to her?"

"Sure, Grimes," Jared said. "Why?"

"Thet's a lot of dough ta toss away."

"Well, it's gonna buy her some time, so shut up about it."

Grimes chuckled. "Okay. Lover boy."

A few miles down the road, McGraw pulled his horse to a stop.

"What's the matter, Boss, forgot somethin' back there?"

"Nope," the ramrod said. "It's somethin' I gotta do, Tug. An' ifn I don't do it I won't be able look at my ugly kisser in the mirror. It's a matter of honor."

"Is it what I think it is?"

"Most likely, Tug. You want a part of it?"

"Hell, yeah," Tug Grimes said. "Maybe the rest of the boys, Henry, Bradley and O'Toole want a piece of it, too, don't ya think?"

"Yeah," McGraw said. "I guess I was getting' a little greedy, wantin' ta have all the fun ta myself. C'mon, let's ride."

They rode fast towards the Box R Ranch. A full moon above made the going easy. They came pounding into the yard and quickly dismounted. McGraw took Jared aside.

"Jared, this ain't yer play. All I want you ta do is watch over the lady. Kin ya do thet?"

"Are you sure? You might need an extra gun."

"No. I'm callin' the shots on this one, Jared. Thanks, anyway. You jest take care of Miss Restin. Will ya do thet?"

"I will, Stoke."

"Thet's all I ask."

McGraw and Grimes went into the bunkhouse. Jared went up onto the porch and eased his way quietly into the living room and lay on the couch where he had spent the previous night. His blanket was still there.

A few minutes later he heard the Box R cowboys ride out into the night. Erica came down in her night robe, with a shawl over her shoulders.

"What's going on, Mr. Jared?" she asked.

She came up to him. She yawned and put a hand on his arm. She had been asleep and wasn't completely awake at this late hour.

"I don't know, ma'am," Jared said.

"Was that our boys riding out at this late hour?"

"Yes, ma'am. It was."

"Where are they going?"

"I don't know."

"I can't sleep. Can I stay down here with you?"

"Yes, ma'am."

"Should I make coffee?"

Jared nodded and Erica went into the kitchen.

Jared looked out into the empty yard. The bunkhouse was dark and it was starting to snow.

18.

It was snowing hard when the six Box R cowboys rode up a rise close to the Triangle D compound. They sat in their saddles looking down at the bunkhouse. A light was on inside, as well as inside the huge, two-story, white clapboard ranch house nearby.

"Damn," Tug Grimes said. "He's livin' high on the hog, ain't he?"

"Thet's a helluva lot of house fer one hombre," Pages Henry commented.

"He throws a shindig most every week," McGraw replied. "He brings in girls from the Blue Moon Saloon."

"What's the next move, Boss?" Charcoal Bradley asked.

McGraw looked over at Henry. "You got the rope?"

Henry patted the rope on his saddle horn. "Yep."

"We'll walk on in, then," the big ramrod said.

He dismounted and stood by his horse a moment then rubbed its neck and ears.

"Go home, old friend," McGraw said and slapped the animal on the rump to get it moving. It ran off out of sight.

The others dismounted and did the same, watching as their mounts disappeared into the shroud of falling whiteness.

They all checked their guns.

"How come we didn't bring Jared?" Puncher Elliot asked.

"He's watchin' out fer Miss Restin, like I told him ta do," McGraw said. "Anyway, this is our dance, not his."

The others nodded.

McGraw took the first fateful step and led them down the rise towards the ranch house fifty yards away. It felt colder now and the swirling snow made it hard to see ahead. A dog barked over by the barn. They stopped for a moment then went on.

As they came into the yard one of the Triangle D cowboys came from the bunkhouse half dressed. He shivered and ran back around to the outhouse, never noticing the intruders thirty feet away.

McGraw led them quickly to the house and up the porch steps. The cold boards creaked under their combined weight.

A voice from the house called out, "Is that you, Malone?"

"Yeah!" McGraw answered. He opened the door and quickly went in.

The others came close behind.

They went down the hallway and turned right to where they saw Denvers sitting in his study at his desk. He saw them, too. For a moment he looked confused, then realized who they were.

"McGraw!" Denvers yelled and started to reach into the top drawer of his desk.

As Denvers pulled out the gun, McGraw leaped upon him and the two went crashing on the floor in a tangled heap. The gun went off, blowing a hole in the desk. Puncher Elliot ran over and slammed a fist into the rancher's face, knocking him half unconscious. Henry rushed in to help. They all picked Denvers up and carried him out of the study into the hall.

"Grimes, you hold the door! Bradley, you and O'Toole back him up!" McGraw yelled.

At that moment there was a rush of feet outside.

"Colonel Denvers, sir, are you okay?" someone yelled.

Grimes fanned off six shots into the door. As he reloaded, O'Toole and Bradley poured six more into it. They heard groans and screaming out on the porch.

"Hold the door, men!" McGraw screamed again as they continue to drag Denvers up the stairs to the balcony on the second landing.

When they got to the balcony, Henry slipped the noose-end of the rope over the Colonel's head. He struggled and kicked out. Elliot smashed him in the face again.

"Why?" the rancher screamed. "Why?"

"Fer the cold-blooded murder of Jim Restin," McGraw growled. "An' may yer rotten soul burn in hell."

McGraw and Henry held the rope as Puncher Elliot lifted the big rancher up and slid him over the balcony railing. His screams turned into a guttural hissing as he dangled three feet above the floor below. In a few moments he stopped struggling.

"We need help down here, Boss!" Grimes yelled up the stairs.

"Hang on, Tug!" McGraw hollered back.

They tied the rope to the bannister, ran down the stairs and put out the light in the study. Standing quietly in the dark they waited for what they knew was about to come.

"How many are out there, you think?" Bradley asked.

"Sounds like about twenty or more," Grimes answered.

McGraw chuckled.

"Shucks, thet about makes it even, don't it, Punch?"

"Hell, yeah, Stoke," Puncher Elliot chuckled. "I feel sorry fer them bastards!"

There was a moment of silence, then all hell broke loose. Bullets began to pour into the hallway through the door and windows of the study.

"Who the hell are we, boys?" McGraw bellowed like an enraged bull as the bullets came in at them.

"We're the Box R!" they yelled as one.

"Then, give 'em hell, boys!"

O'Toole began to sing the Irish battle hymn, "The Rising of the Moon." His voice started soft as a whisper then gathered strength and rose clear and loud against the barking of the guns.

19.

On February 25, 1886, a banner headline appeared in the Haverston Herald that read:

RANGE WAR!

Three nights ago, cowboys of the small Box R ranch and those of the much larger Triangle D met in a clash of raw gunfire.

According to survivors, the Box R cowboys, Pages Henry, Charcoal Bradley, Tonsils O'Toole, Puncher Elliot and Tug Grimes, led by the Box R ramrod, Stoker McGraw, made a sneak night attack on Colonel Denvers' ranch house some time after midnight.

Alerted by the sound of gunfire, the Triangle D cowboys tried to rescue the Colonel but were met with a withering fusillade of gunfire from the Box R men who had barricaded themselves in the ranch house. The Triangle D cowboys made several frontal attacks. Each attack cost them high casualties.

Unable to penetrate the Box R defenses, the Triangle D cowboys finally surrounded the mansion and poured gunfire into it all through the night. The Triangle D cowboys said they thought they heard someone singing off and on in the mansion, until the last attack at dawn.

At daylight, after an hour of silence, the Triangle D men made a last attempt rush on the mansion. Inside they found all the Box R men dead. Colonel Denvers was found hanging by a rope from the second story bannister. He had not been shot, only hung. Fifteen Triangle D men lay dead.

Just below this story was a short one that read:

STARTLING CONFESSION!

Haverston's marshal, Tom Tolliver, has shown this newspaper a startling confession by the former ramrod of the Triangle D ranch that accuses owner Colonel Frank Denvers of hiring professional gunslingers from Wichita to come to Haverston to kill the Box R cowboys and the owner of the Box R Ranch, Miss Erica Restin, as well. The Colonel, as we reported previously, had killed Miss Restin's brother James in a duel at the Gentlemen's Club, not long ago.

On February 26, 1886, an article in the Haverston Herald read:

RANCH TO BE AUCTIONED!

The ranch of deceased owner Colonel Frank Denvers is being offered at auction in three smaller parcels. Denvers had no living relatives. The Triangle D was once the largest thriving ranch in the area.

...

Clay Jared and Erica Restin stood on the platform of the Haverston Junction depot next to the train heading to Wichita. From there she was going to Chicago to visit some friends and then on to New York to meet her father and mother. They would take an ocean cruise and finally go back to London after spending some time in Italy. Her father's lawyers were handling the sale of the Box R Ranch.

The March Kansas wind was sassy as usual and blew snow in their faces and nipped at their ears.

Jared chuckled. "Italy will be warm."

"Yes," Erica said. She looked around. "I'll miss this savage land called Kansas with its beautiful people."

Suddenly she began to weep.

"Oh God, Clay! Why did they do it? Why did they throw their lives away like that? I'm not worth it."

"We don't have much out here in the way of education and money, but we do have one thing. It's a code we live by, Erica. To men, like the Colonel, the code means nothing. It isn't real to them."

"But to Mr. McGraw, it was real, wasn't it?"

"Yes. Very real."

"I'll miss them all, you know. Someday I might write a book about them. And you, too, Clay." She wiped her eyes.

"That would be nice, Erica."

"I have Mr. Bradley's sketch book. I'm in it."

"I know. I saw it. I'm in it too," Clay said. He paused a moment, then asked, "That book that Pages Henry had?"

"*Moby Dick*?"

"Yes, *Moby Dick*. Was he really reading it?"

"Yes, he was. He could read very well," Erica said. She smiled and looked off into the distance. "I'll miss Mr. O'Toole's beautiful voice."

"Yes. I will too."

Erica started to sob again.

"Oh, God, Clay! I loved them so much! Hold me, please."

She came into his arms and clung to him. He kissed her and held her tight. They heard the engine whistle blow and people started boarding the train. He let her go. They looked into each other's eyes, he nodded and she got onto the train.

It moved slowly north towards Wichita and in a few moments the caboose went by, picking up speed. Jared watched the train get smaller and smaller until it was a dot and then nothing.

He stood there a while then walked over to his horse and rubbed its neck and ears. It nudged him and he mounted up and headed for the Box R. It was still daylight and he had time for one last look.

He got there by mid-afternoon, dismounted and looked around.

It was strange to see all the emptiness, hear all the quietness, and feel the echoes of the ghosts of the Box R cowboys. Everything was gone. The corral was empty and no chickens ran around squawking. No dog chased a cat. The windows of the ranch house looked like vacant, non-seeing eyes. A curtain stirred as if an invisible hand had moved it. Jared smiled. Was the spirit of James haunting the place? The barn seemed larger, for some reason. It was now but an empty shell. Everything had been auctioned off.

Jared went into the bunkhouse. The weak winter light cast shadows across the empty cots. He sat down on Pages Henry's bunk and rolled a cigarette.

"Let me know how it turns out," Jared had said, in regards to *Moby Dick.*

"I sure will," Pages Henry had said.

But he never did, and never would, now.

Jared could still remember the feel of Erica kiss. He chuckled.

"Good luck, Miss Erica Restin," he said out loud, as if she could hear him.

Suddenly he felt very tired. He'd sat on his bunk to rest. He would miss the cowboys of the Box R. By this time tomorrow Erica would be miles away and he would be moving on.

Later he would ride into Haverston Junction and try some of the son of a gun stew at the beanery there. It couldn't be any worse than the old Box R cook, Henry Finley's. He chuckled, wondering who Henry was poisoning now.

Outside of the bunkhouse the wind began to howl and it began to snow again.

The End.

About the Author

As a young boy growing up in the city, R. Annan never passed up a chance to see a Western movie. His heroes were Buck Jones, Johnny Mack Brown, Wild Bill Elliot and John Wayne, to name a few. As an adult, he often wondered where his love of Westerns came from. Perhaps it has something to do with his grandfather, John L. Annan, who was a cowboy from Helena, Montana, in days of old.

A Note from the Author

Thank you for reading my book. If you enjoyed it, would you please consider rating and reviewing it? I'd enjoy your feedback. Thank you!

Look for other books to appear soon.